To Tilou,
well done & best
of all luck in the
future.

J.A.Clarke.

By the same author

The Elementary Cases of Sherlock Holmes

Watson's
Last Case

Ian Alfred Charnock

**BREESE
BOOKS
LONDON**

First published in 2000 by
Breese Books Ltd
164 Kensington Park Road, London W11 2ER, England

ISBN: 0 947 533 923

Typeset in 11½/14½pt Caslon by
Ann Buchan (Typesetters), Middlesex
Printed and bound in Great Britain
by Itchen Printers Limited, Southampton

Publisher's Note

In *The Elementary Cases of Sherlock Holmes*, 'young' Stamford told of some of Mr Sherlock Holmes's early cases. Now, in *Watson's Last Case*, Stamford reveals what happened after Watson had joined up with his old service in 1914. Stamford also tells us about his own youthful adventures and indiscretions, and in what he (being both a surgeon and a man who could never resist a bad pun) calls 'A Scholar's Appendix', Stamford gives some details about those fascinating aspects of Holmes's life which so intrigue students of the world's first consulting detective.

Contents

Part One

Doctor's Orders

'Whatever have you been doing with yourself, Watson?'

From *A Study in Scarlet*

In the Bar of the Criterion

Well do I remember meeting John H. Watson MD in the Criterion bar all those years ago. As Watson himself observed we had never been particular cronies at the hospital — for a start he was a three-quarter (which was no easy position in those days, and he took on an even more demanding role in his later playing days, which was to prove very influential on the subsequent development of Rugby Union Football, not that the modest biographer ever mentioned any of this) and I was a pack man; front row in fact. Also we were several years apart in age. Nonetheless I had always got on with him. He was always very fair and kept his dressers in order. Thus it came as no surprise to learn that he had joined the army after taking his degree. However, it was certainly a surprise to see the state that he was in that day at the Criterion.

At first I did not really recognize him and so remained in my corner seat and merely observed him as one would any interesting stranger.

I noticed the stiff arm, the slightly unsteady walk which in conjunction with the thinness of his flesh covering — he looked as though he was wearing an elder, larger brother's clothes — all confirmed my diagnosis that here was a wounded soldier, not a drunken one. But was it Watson? The deep tan and thinness put me out but witnessing his solidity despite his injuries and privations as he stood at the bar steadfast as ever convinced me. I jumped up from my seat and tapped him on the shoulder. To my surprise, and pleasure, he recognized me instantly and greeted me like a brother despite the already noted slightness of our acquaintance. In truth we were brothers after a fashion, not just of the Hippocratic Oath but in our loneliness. I was delighted to see him. That was always the effect that he had on people in distress whether they knew him well or hardly at all. He would have passed with high honours the test that a much later British general of Norman stock devised, viz. 'Is he the sort of man you can rely on to take into the bush with you?' Most definitely he was.

My loneliness was self-imposed as a result of some foolishness of youth which I am pleased to say that my friend did not reveal in his writings and which I do not intend to do even now.

Watson's loneliness was also self-imposed, not that he had anything to be ashamed of. He had made quite a few friends in London during his hospital and Blackheath rugby days — one must never underestimate his qualities — but I assume that he kept out of their way because he was not really up to much socializing (young doctors of the rugby fraternity can be rather boisterous) and also because he no doubt felt that on eleven shillings and sixpence a day he was hardly in a position to pay his way in society or reciprocate hospitality. How he paid for our luncheon at the Holborn I cannot say, neither did I think it correct to enquire.

However, all of this is of little consequence now compared with the great service that I was able to render Mr Sherlock Holmes which was, of course, to introduce him to

his — I was going to say his Jonathan, or Oliver, or Gib-
bon, or even Boswell but all are inadequate. Suffice to say
Holmes now had his Watson.

My part was now over and I disappear completely from
the scene never to be mentioned again even in passing.
However that may be on the surface, there is more to young
Stamford than meets the eye.

On Active Service

A signal sounded and complete strangers embraced. In the Circus there was dancing in the streets and unrestrained singing. In the Square the lions looked on in dignified silence as crowds swayed around them to the accompaniment of patriotic songs. The whole of London was glistening with the tears of happiness, relief and remembrance. It was the eleventh hour of the eleventh day of the eleventh month, 1918.

The Criterion bar was awash with bonhomie. The Zeppelins, Somme and Passchendaele were already only a nightmare — but three among many that would haunt a generation to their graves. I stood four square to the bar my hand gripping the rail as I ordered a large planter's punch. I still wore my naval surgeon's uniform, the thickness of its cloth proof against the biting November morning. 'And another for any navy man, royal or merchant, who should ask for a bungyereye,' I added placing my last £5 note on the bar with a conspiratorial wink. Meadows, the barman, murmured a discreet 'Of course, sir,' and went about his business.

I looked around me at the men gathered in the bar. All were in uniform, but the khaki was not drab on this first morning; it was enlivened by the faces of its occupants now so alive and animated after the last four years of unimaginable, unfathomable degradation. There were also groups of women in the bar — an unthinkable state of affairs four short/long years ago. The war had brought unexpected changes, many of which I have still not caught up with. In days gone by the only women to be found unescorted in such places would have been harlots but here in the Criterion bar their starched nurses' uniforms concealed any differences between heiresses and whores, haves and have nots, giving them all the appearance of angels of mercy. Their cheeks were as rosy as Worcesters, their eyes as bright as pips, their lips as red as cherries, and their complexions as glowing with life as a healthy newborn babe. I smiled a quiet knowing smile to myself and inwardly laughed. Here was I, 'Young' Stamford rhapsodising over girls who were young enough, in some cases at least, to be my grandchildren. Yet still I smiled. History had made a bit player of me before, but now my old age had made me into an observer. 'Stumpy' Stamford had survived and each breath was more poignant as a result.

Just as I toasted a group of weary but elated Devonshires I felt a hand rest on my shoulder. It was at once firm, friendly and unmistakable. I almost mouthed the words of greeting before I had turned.

'My word, it's young Stamford,' said a voice from my past. I turned and saw a stranger. My breath left my body and my brows knitted as I attempted to put a name to the face. 'As thin as a lathe and as brown as a nut,' prompted my new companion. Our eyes met and a thousand wonderful feelings passed between us.

'It's John H. Watson.'

My companion smiled, 'Indeed so, young Stamford.'

Spontaneously we hugged as though we were brothers, once prodigal now united. Some of the Devonshires had seen us and witnessing our ecstasy applauded. Our warmth became self-conscious. We ran a gauntlet of hearty back-slapping and 'Well done, the men,' as we retired to a corner seat where some thirty-eight years before I had sat and seen a hero 'as thin as a lathe and brown as a nut' come into the Criterion and order a sherry.

At first we could only look at each other. We could not believe it. We had survived! To be young must have been very heaven that day but to be reunited with old friends believed deceased was an even sweeter joy. We chuckled at each other and starting speaking at the same time. We then both stopped at the same time. After two more false starts Watson took command and asked, 'How did your war go?'

I quickly outlined my work on the convoys, the chief memories being the bitter cold and the boredom.

'Is that why you have a full set [of fungus] now? I did not recognize you at first and observed you from this corner seat for several minutes before I dared to chance my arm. Not only did I have to mentally shave you but I had to take your hat off as well.'

He answered my puzzled look. 'The red hair with the lock of carrot. No-one that I have ever met has had such hair.' I then realized that I must have taken my hat off when we cheered the eleventh hour.

'I would have been in trouble if the years had taken your hair as well as your youth, Stamford.'

We both laughed. I was about to offer a toast to red hair when a young Royal Flying Corps, or should I say RAF chap, bumped into our table. He steadied himself and said, 'You command more by your gravity than any grey hair.' We chortled and suggested an alternative corruption of his 'Othello'. 'No matter,' he replied. 'My apologies to the fouled anchor,' he said saluting me. 'And please forgive me, sir,' he said to Watson, standing to attention and saluting.

Despite his obvious discomfort Watson rose and reciprocated the gesture. In a moment the scene had been dispelled but the impression endured. I studied Watson. He was very thin and despite the brownness of his burnt skin he had a strange pallor about him, a curious mixture of green and yellow which extended to the whites of his eyes. Watson was a sick man. The RAF man had gone and Watson had resumed his seat. What had he been up to?

'What have I been up to?' He smiled in answer to the unspoken question that was obviously clear to read on my features. 'Would that I could tell you and that you would be able to believe me.'

'You are no liar, Watson. Of course I would believe you.'

'But we were talking about you, Stamford. Surely there was more to convoy work than cold and boredom?'

'Oh yes. There was fear and there was work.'

'Were you at Jutland or the Dogger Bank in your travels?'

'No. That was a job for the Senior Service, not the red duster.'

Watson sipped his drink. I had to take the initiative and try to make him talk about himself. As Holmes had had occasion to say more than once, Watson had never given himself sufficient credit for his own abilities. I adopted a light-hearted approach.

'Enough of the old sea-dog, what about the old soldier? If I were to combine my skills as a ship's surgeon with Holmes's powers of deduction, I would say that you have been doing your bit for king and country. You have been wounded and your theatre was the Frontier.'

Watson smiled at the mention of his old friend.

'Perhaps you will explain?'

'It's easy: your tan is from a sun that we seldom find penetrating London's dismal clouds or France's mud so you have been to hotter climes. Your bearing shows you as a military man despite the fact that you are not in uniform under your army greatcoat. That flyer assumed you were of high rank into the bargain.'

'But the wound and the Frontier?'

'I'm coming to that. You are too old, begging your pardon, Watson, as I am only several years your junior, to have been at the front, therefore you have been showing the flag and recruiting in your old stamping ground of India and the Frontier. You were an ideal choice. As to the wound, your arm is a little stiff and you are not the right colour around the gills. Howzat?'

'Not out, I'm afraid, Stamford. I have not been wounded. True, I am a little stiff-jointed at the moment, but that is an English November, not wounds received at the front; this time, that is. Also, I have not been to India recruiting, but to the front in . . . But no, it is too crowded here. We must go somewhere else. What about . . .'

'The Holborn, of course!' I interjected. 'I owe you a meal. Admittedly it's taken me thirty-eight years to get round to it but at least you cannot fault my memory or accuse me of trying to duck my debts.'

'Well, I wasn't . . .' started Watson, but I was too enthusiastic to brook any prevarication.

'No, no, I insist. This time I must pay and you shall have as much Beaune as you could wish.' With that we stepped out of the Criterion and into the swaying masses thronging Piccadilly Circus singing 'Auld Lang Syne' for the tenth time already. For a moment Watson staggered in the crush. I put an arm around him and gripped his belt tightly. 'Ah, the old front row grip, I see,' observed Watson, his eyes twinkling. After much toing and froing in search of a cab, Watson tugged my sleeve and shouted above the din, 'I think the Holborn may be overbooked today. Come back to my place.'

'Is that Queen Anne Street? Or did you finally take over in Harley Street?'

'Indeed I did, but I sold out when I retired at the start of the war, so really it's neither.'

'Where to then?'

'221B Baker Street.'

It was with a thrill that I heard those words. What adventure would be in store for me there? After a journey made longer by the crowds of jostling revellers we arrived at the famous address. It was the first time that I had been there and I approached the door with something akin to reverence. Once inside, Watson soon had everything under control. The lunch was ordered, the fire stoked up, great-coat exchanged for a dressing gown, pipe lit and armchair occupied, as I poured the drinks and grappled with the gasogene. 'Oh, don't bother with that, Stamford. Use the syphon, it's much better. Only Holmes could ever work that old thing.'

As I poured I looked around at the sitting room which had been the starting point of so many wonderful adventures that I had followed religiously no matter where I was. It looked just as Watson had described it in his famous stories — perhaps a trifle tidier. Watson informed me as I gave him his drink that he had restored it as far as possible to its former glories but Holmes had taken his papers and voluminous commonplace books with him so that the room had lost some of its earlier clutter. In the corner was a collection of chemistry equipment but it was collecting dust from lack of use. A violin lay on its side, but as Watson said, it was not the original 55/- Stradivarius. Understandably Holmes had taken that with him to Sussex. A Persian slipper still contained tobacco which I replenished with some of my genuine Ship's, much to Watson's delight.

Before long our meal appeared as did several bottles of

Beaune still shrouded in a thick layer of cellar dust. Watson winked, 'A good soldier always has something in reserve.'

When we had finished our meal we returned to our armchairs on either side of the fire. Watson sat in thought for several minutes as though trying to resolve a problem. At last he reached a decision and fixed me with a solemn face. 'Do you know, Stamford,' he began, 'I knew that you would be in the Criterion today. For some reason I felt that you just had to be, although the fungus camouflage fooled me for a moment. Yes, odd isn't it, but one gets strangely lucid about certain things at my time of life. There are several things that I want you to do for me if it's not too much trouble.'

'Anything, Watson old chap, you know that.'

'Well done, Stamford. I knew I could rely on you. In that briefcase over there you will find twelve cases of Sherlock Holmes in one of my books. I want you to go and see my literary agent and get them published. They are some of the oddest cases that we were ever involved in but there are several cases that mean a lot to me because they reveal more of Holmes the man than most of my other efforts. Their publication will put Holmes into some sort of proper perspective. Unfortunately I have only fully completed four of them but the others only need a little burnishing to be ready and the notes are very full.'

'Why don't you finish them now the war's over?'

Watson smiled, 'Oh, I may, but you know how things pile up. I just wanted to be sure that you would be able to lend a helping hand if need be. Another drink?'

I ordered another absently — I was worried about Watson. But, as if to prove that my fears were groundless, he bounded across to the drinks, topped up our glasses and with a deft flick brought the gasogene into life. 'Well, that's something I seem to have learnt from Holmes.'

'What of Sherlock Holmes?' I asked as Watson regained his seat.

'I wrote to him the other day asking permission to publish. I expect his wire at any moment; he never wrote if he could wire. I think he still prefers it to the telephone. He will say yes, as long as he is not disturbed. No doubt making more observations on the queen bee to add to his work.'

'Have you seen him at all recently?'

'No, not since the Von Bork episode at the start of the war.'

'Do you know how he is?'

'I only know that he gets crippling bouts of rheumatism but then don't we all?' At that a moment a bout seemed to take hold of Watson as he gripped his shoulder. 'Blast that bullet and London in November.' After a few moments he seemed to recover but despite his tan he looked pale and drawn.

'Are you all right, old chap?'

'Fine, fine, Stamford young fella. Now where was I? Holmes. Oh yes, that's right. All the other cases I was involved in are in my despatch box at Cox and Co, Charing Cross — if a Zeppelin didn't drop a bomb on them, that is — and Holmes will decide their future. Which brings me to why I wanted to see you of all people, Stamford. You too know of several cases from the inside as it were, that were before my time. Would you tell me about them? Do you know about the "singular affair of the aluminium crutch"? Who was Ricoletti, and why did Holmes describe his wife as abominable? First you must tell me and then I shall tell you about my adventure at the front.'

It seemed a fair deal to me. Thus throughout the afternoon of that first day of peace I told my old friend about Algernon Berry and Delicia Ogilvy, Matilda Briggs, Olga

Pleshkarova, Mrs Farintosh and the opal tiara, Ricoletti and his wife, the extraordinary Tarleton murders, and finally, Vanberry. He never ceased to be amazed by the phenomenal abilities of his old friend despite the fact that he had seen him at work from close quarters on hundreds of occasions. Perhaps that had been part of the attraction for Holmes. As well as his goodness and honesty, Watson was also an enthusiastic admirer of Holmes's gifts and no matter what might be said to the contrary Holmes did have a streak of vanity in his character, particularly at the beginning. In return, Watson asked if there was any particular case that I wished to hear about. There was only one but when he had filled in the details and explained the connections between the politician, the lighthouse and the trained cormorant, it was my turn to be amazed.

'Strangely enough,' rejoined Watson, 'it was my part in that case — passive as it was really — that brought about my adventures in Palestine . . .'

'Palestine?' I gasped in wonder.

'Why yes. Surely you had deduced that already? Still, as I was saying, even the War Cabinet conceded that I could be trusted to carry out the mission after my role in that convoluted affair was revealed to them. Particularly as two of them were related to the politician in question. The way they behaved I wondered if they were related to the cormorant. However, as I was to discover it proved to be a backhanded compliment.'

'But Palestine, at your age?'

'At my age.'

'How?'

'Mycroft.'

'Then why not Holmes himself?'

'He could not be spared.'

'So he has not been simply observing bees these last four

years?'

'Presumably not.'

'But why not anybody else?'

'I was the only one who was trusted by all.'

'All?'

'Indeed. But before I continue I must warn you that I swore never to reveal my role in the Middle East. No general's memoirs or historian's account of the war in the desert will ever mention Dr John H. Watson and nor must you until the War Office releases its own papers. Is that understood?'

'Perhaps you would prefer not to say anything?'

Watson pondered again for a moment as he had done earlier but he soon looked up and said, 'No, I made my mind up earlier, yesterday in fact. I must tell my side. It is only fair.'

'Why not write it down and leave it in your despatch box?'

'No time for that I'm afraid, but let's get on, the street lamps are already long lit and this historic day will soon be no more if we delay.'

Watson refilled his pipe and coughed throatily.

'You must know if you have followed my accounts of the cases of Mr Sherlock Holmes that in recent years I have taken a great interest in motor cars and have owned several in the past ten years or so. My favourite has always been the cars manufactured by the Rolls-Royce Company. I have owned several and have been considered quite an enthusiast in my own way. When the war broke out I tried to enlist in the Medical Corps but I was rejected on the grounds of my age; nevertheless a friend of mine got in touch with me and thought of a way around it. I say a friend, he was more an acquaintance whom I had met at several functions. He had got together a group of fellow Rolls-Royce enthusiasts and they were going out to the front in Flanders in their cars. As fate would have it I could not join them then because I was involved in a very important medical case which involved the royal families of two of the most powerful countries in the world. The case was long and involved calling for a great deal of discretion. My time was fully occupied until the very end of 1917.

'Eventually I returned to London, my work complete although I feared even more for my patient's life, but it was out of my hands by then. My name was on the reserve list for the Medical Corps in France and I expected to be on my way to Flanders by spring 1918 at the latest. However, events had overtaken me and I received a note to call upon Mycroft Holmes at the Diogenes Club. We met in the committee room as we knew we would not be disturbed there — those unclubbable fellows never held a committee meeting to my knowledge.

'There he outlined my duties to me. It was a call to my patriotism and I could not disobey. It is from that meeting that I date my loss of innocence in this world of ours.'

Watson paused, gripped by some great emotion.

Suddenly he grasped his shoulder again and coughed a terrible cough that seemed to shake his entire being. I rushed to him but he signalled me back to my chair. He took a deep swallow of his drink and asked me for a refill.

'Excuse me, Stamford, but these fits have come and gone recently. Let us hope that that is the end of them for today.' He composed himself and continued.

'You know Mycroft of course. When we met he was grosser than ever and the years were crowding in on him. His voice revealed a bronchial disorder but his eyes still retained that far away, introspective look that I had first noticed in the case of the "Greek Interpreter" when we had originally met.

'He soon came to the point. "What do you know of near Eastern politics and the Ottoman Empire?"

'Apart from Metternich's phrase beaten into me at school about Turkey being the "sick man of Europe"* I had to confess, very little.

' "Well, perhaps that is as well," replied my host.

' "All you need to know is that Turkey must fall now that she has thrown in her lot with our German cousins. We have another front in the Holy Land that needs very careful handling. The entry into Jerusalem was a major morale-booster for our troops on the Western Front and Allenby has shown himself to be a great talent after all. He has been able to orchestrate his forces as diverse as regular army, navy, merchant ships, aeroplanes, Indians, Australians and Arab irregulars as though he understands why a field marshal has a baton as his symbol. Do you know him? No? It is of little moment.

' "Not only have you heard of the fall of Jerusalem to our latter day Lionheart but you may also have heard of the fall of Akaba despite your recent state of incommunicado. It was taken from the Turkish regular army by a group of Arab irregulars. The British Royal Navy was not ten miles away when this group of thirty-five skirt-wearing desert dwellers against all orders of their British superiors broke camp and went on a forced camel ride of some two hundred miles through uncharted wasteland in order to take the Turks by surprise from behind. As it turns out they were right to do so. All the Turks' weapons were trained on the sea so that they were completely exposed on the land flank. The Turks surrendered without a struggle, and the Arabs only lost two men in an earlier skirmish. The leader of

---

*Either Watson did not have a good history teacher or he was not an attentive pupil: the phrase was coined by Nicholas I of Russia.

these Arabs was a former archaeologist from Oxford whom they call 'Aurens' but is better known as Colonel T.E. Lawrence. It is with him that your assignment begins."

'"With him? The man seems more than capable to me." '

'"Indeed he is very capable. Almost too capable. He is going to be a hero and heroes can be very dangerous. After the fall of Akaba he went back to GHQ in his Arab garment — barefoot, too — and on the way refused to salute any officers. When asked by the military police to explain who he was he said that he was in the Meccan army. When they said it did not exist and certainly did not know the uniform he asked them if they would recognize a Montenegrin dragoon if they saw one.

'"You might think it humorous, Dr Watson, but the Eastern Question has been the ruin of many a diplomat by its sheer complexity. We cannot allow any young Alexander to go cutting Gordian knots without regard for the consequences. He must be watched and influenced to keep to the government's line to keep his Arabs in order and subject to Allenby.

'"You have been chosen, Dr Watson, because you are one of the most reliable men in the Empire as you have recently proved on your last case. Not only that, you have experience of hot climates, you are well up on nervous disorders and this new psychology — skills which you may well need in dealing with this man if reports of his behaviour are to be believed. You were my brother's companion for twenty-three years so you should be used to dealing with eccentrics. In conclusion I would point out that I think that he would listen to you above all others, apart possibly from Sherlock but he is too busy to be spared at the moment."

'"But why do you think that I could influence him?" '

'"Because among his baggage he has various books, the most thumbed being the *Morte d'Arthur* and the *Memoirs of Sherlock Holmes*."

'"I will do it, of course." '

'"Good, good. I knew I could rely on you, doctor. The other thing that strongly recommends you is that you have a Rolls-Royce."

'"How does that recommend me?" '

'"Don't think that I don't know about your desire to join up with a certain duke's private detachment of armoured Rolls-Royces. After Flanders they were posted to Cairo where they have distinguished themselves against the Senussi. Colonel Lawrence was very impressed by them and has been able to take over the duke's Rolls-Royces. I am sure that he could do with another, if you get my meaning, Dr Watson. Thus you will be able to join up with Colonel Lawrence and exert a calming influence on him before he goes too far. Your papers will arrive tomorrow and you will be aboard your ship the day after. Good luck."

'I left the Diogenes full of elation. Action at last. Useful at last. But when I got back here the more I thought about it the more I found it somehow distasteful. Really I was nothing more than a spy on a fellow British soldier. This was not my idea of fighting. However, when I thought along those lines I kept reminding myself of Mycroft's final words to me as I left the club that my mission was vital to the safety and morale of the entire British Empire. If Allenby could succeed where the Crusaders of Richard the Lionheart had failed by conquering the Holy Land and turning it into a British sphere of influence with all that entailed — peace and progress — then not only Britain but Mankind would be the winner. With that logic I could not argue. It became my duty to carry out this mission successfully. It was also to be my very secret duty and I was to go under an alias for the others only revealing my identity to Lawrence. It appeared that my recent medical case might have made me enemies and my whereabouts would be under surveillance from foreign unfriendly agents.

'In two days I was on my way to Egypt with my Rolls safely stowed below deck with a new brass name plate on the driver's door — "Bull Pup".

'Why "Bull Pup", Stamford? Two reasons. Apparently the duke had given his cars names and they all began with "B" such as "Bloodhound" and "Blast". My name was in memory of the bull pup I had kept when I was in the hotel after returning from Afghanistan. When I moved in with Holmes to 221B I brought the little chap with me but the poor creature must have got confused about where he was. One day he got out and tried to find his way back to the hotel. Need I spell out what happened to him in London's traffic congestion in his confusion? Poor little fellow. I never had a dog again — just couldn't face it after what had happened to him.

'Now where was I? Oh yes, Egypt. What a magnificent civilization that must have been. Their buildings dwarf modern man. We British still have a lot to learn about Empires if we take the Pharaohs as our spirit guides. However, there was no time for sightseeing, Lawrence was far away near the Jordan and I had to catch up with him.

'I first got to Beersheba to present my compliments to General Allenby. What a fine figure of a man he was. Tall and powerful, healthy and impeccably turned out despite the heat, sand and dust. We discussed my mission and he confessed that he understood London's concern all those miles away but Colonel Lawrence had been through a lot and he had never let the side down yet. So Allenby obviously felt that Lawrence could be relied upon to do his duty.

'Next I spoke to B-----. He was a keen young man helping to set up the Rolls-Royce cars. He spoke in awe of both the cars and Colonel Lawrence. First he told me about the duke's Royal Automobile Volunteers and their tangles with the Senussi. Apparently their Sheikh had taken some shipwrecked sailors prisoner and was holding them in what he thought was an inaccessible part of the desert. The duke and his cohorts thought differently and went over two hundred miles across the desert where they liberated the sailors. They then pursued the Senussi to their even more isolated stronghold and after a long gun battle they completely routed them. Not one man or car was lost. This was more like it, I thought.

'He then told me about Colonel Lawrence. How highly strung he seemed these days. They had first met when B----- was on sentry duty. Colonel Lawrence had just materialized out of the night with his thirty bodyguards. "Don't wake the boys," he had said. "It's quite all right. I'm Lawrence." He then had a talk with the officer commanding but as he left he did not forget to ask the sentry's name and wish him well. B----- said that he had felt inspired by him. A sort of Nelson touch from the poop deck of a ship of the desert, I suppose you could say.

'But on the other hand, when they had blown up a bridge a huge piece of masonry and metal missed Lawrence by inches but instead of being shocked or whatever, he simply giggled like a girl. He seemed to be getting reckless somehow. Putting himself in danger for some reason. Forcing himself to the limits of his endurance. Everyone admired him but many were afraid for him.

'Next I spoke to H-----. He was very understanding about Colonel Lawrence and spoke of him like a brother and not in the awed, reverential tones of B-----. He told me of the occasion when Lawrence had come to see him to complain bitterly about his position. He had spoken out against what he saw as simply playing a role, acting as the leader of someone else's rebellion which involved daily deception, posturing and preaching in alien speech, while behind it all was fraud and dishonour. Would the Arabs be really free and self-governing when the war was over as the Allies had promised them? As he himself had promised them? Lawrence had said that he felt his will leaving him, he had been under strain too long and now with a price on his head of £20,000 he found himself tempted to take on more danger in order to prove himself. He had even confessed to a fear of being on his own in case he was finally blown away and his empty soul dispersed like so much sand. H----- agreed that Lawrence needed my help very soon.

'Next I went to see the Intelligence staff. D----- curtly asked me if I read the newspapers. Needless to say I found his manner impudent and answered that since arriving back in London at the end of 1917 I had not had time to read an up-to-date edition so I was a little out of touch with the latest court circulars. With that he tossed a bundle of cuttings onto the table between us. All were full of reports concerning the new revolutionary government of Russia which had been publishing the diplomatic papers of the ousted tsar's foreign office. The reports were full of secret negotiations which "betrayed the people" or "exposed the proletariat (whatever that was) to the machinations of imperialist aggression and subversion."

'D----- impatiently directed my attention to certain paragraphs that he had underlined in blue pencil. When I read them I could see clearly why that symbol of the censor had come so readily to D-----'s hand. There was a long exposition of a certain Sykes-Picot Plan that had been drawn up in 1916 by His Majesty's Government and the French by which France would take over Syria and the Lebanon at the fall of the Ottoman Empire and Great Britain would take over Iraq, Transjordan and most of Palestine.

'Now I understood Colonel Lawrence's words in his conversation with H-----, and why he had felt so dishonoured. I then realized how I too was equally dishonoured. So this was the government's line that Mycroft had spoken of. Promise one thing to these wretched Bedouins while all the time preparing to carve up the Ottoman Empire with France. I was numb with shock at this duplicity which was on a personal and national level all in one.

'"Where does that leave Colonel Lawrence?" I asked.'

'"Where indeed?" D----- replied. "It has certainly made his task with the Bedouin far more difficult. I am sure that he can handle the Sherif of Mecca, exalted, cantankerous, old man that he is, but what of Feisel, Tallal of Tafas, Auda abu Tayi and all the other leaders? They are not to be trifled with. Yet Lawrence must keep them sweet or we will be fighting Arabs as well as Turks and only the Kremlin will win."

'"I thought that Russia was our ally."

'"So Russia was, but who is in charge now? Presumably this new Bolshy lot or whatever they call themselves."

'"If it is the Bolsheviki," I replied, "then they have no allies."

'"Indeed so. When they took over in the Winter Palace last November they spouted all manner of things about the French Revolution, workers of the world uniting, and even offering to help other revolutions if the workers rose up against their rulers."

'"Sounds a bit extreme to me."

'"A bit extreme? Good heavens, man, it could destroy the world as we know it if it happens. It has been no secret that ally or not Russia has wanted control of the Dardanelles for years so that she has access to the Mediterranean. We can't have that. They'll be using the Canal next, then where would we be?"

'"Hold on a moment, D-----," I cut in, "these Bolsheviki fellows only took over a few months ago and this Sykes-Picot Plan was drawn up in 1916 according to this report. In other words when Tsar Nicholas was still on the throne. Does that mean that two allies of the triple Entente did not trust the third all along?"

'"A good general guards his back as well as his front, doctor. A lesson Colonel Lawrence taught the Turks at Akaba."

'"This sounds like a whole web of deception to me — with the British Government as culpable as the others. In fact more so considering our reputation for fair play."

'"Fair play? The French have envied us for years, these Bolsheviks don't even know the rules so they can't begin to play fair, and we're at war with our own relatives. How can there be fair play?"

'I was shocked at all this. My whole world was being turned on its head, shaken, and then kicked into touch.

'"How is Colonel Lawrence taking this?" I finally asked.

'"Well might you ask that question. Ever since the Deraa incident he has become somewhat changed."

'"The Deraa incident?"

'"Yes, he was doing an Alfred the Great among the Danes finding out the enemy's strength and disposition when he got caught. He was then brutally beaten and physically abused. He's not been quite the same since. HQ says that you are here to give Colonel Lawrence every support and keep him on the road to Damascus. I think he needs it or this whole theatre could crumble and the glorious conquest of Jerusalem will be merely a footnote in a neglected military history."

'"Where is Lawrence now?"

'"We believe somewhere near Azrak. There's a lot of snow about apparently so we won't be seeing him for a few months, although we have reason to believe that he won a famous victory at Tafileh in January. We shall keep you informed."

'I felt that I was being fobbed off. There was a certain buzz about the place but I could not find anyone who would explain it to me. I sat on "Bull Pup's" running board and watched the sunset.

'As you know, Stamford, sunsets there are different from here. The sun becomes a great blood-orange sponge absorbing all the heat from the earth's crust before there is one final blast of heat and it disappears in a few minutes over the horizon. Those few minutes are like something from another time, another planet far more vibrant than our modern world with its electric lights, trams, vagaries of fashion, and machines. It has the effect of making one contemplate one's existence. Then the stars come out, so bright against the sable velvet of the desert sky. There are no fogs or smoking chimneys to obscure the view. No man-made progress to befuddle the senses. It is as though they are communing with the earth. They even look nearer. It makes you feel a true part in some great plan whose solution is written in the stars waiting to be deciphered like some celestial hieroglyph. I wonder if we shall ever find the solution to the cartouche?'

Watson again fell into thought. I waited a moment but decided to shake him from his musings before he went in too deeply.

'What we need is a sort of Rosetta Stone to give us a clue.'

'Indeed, young Stamford, true,' he remarked, but he was still far away. Presently he returned. 'Excuse me, Stamford, but I was just thinking how beautiful it all was — and is at this very moment as we sit here talking. It will be midnight or thereabouts now over there and over the deserts of Arabia Bedouin will be wrapped in their blankets in sand hollows fashioning dreams from what the stars are telling them. But what can we see from our window? Hardly a thing, only glare and congestion. Halley's Comet could come up Piccadilly and no-one would notice. It is as though we have cut ourselves off from God and nature. What have we forfeited with our civilization?

'However, that is only part of my story although one of the most important parts for me personally. That evening I chatted with C-----, H------, and a couple of the others about Lawrence. All agreed in the broad outlines, but it was in the details that differences started to appear, some like hairline cracks, others more pronounced. They were unanimous in saying that the success of the Arab revolt was largely owing to TE as they called him. He was the inspiration, the willpower, the conciliator, the sheer hard worker of the enterprise. Without him the Bedouin would have soon dissipated their energies in old blood feuds and blind alleys. He gave them direction and a dogged resolution when the going got tough.

'It was when it came to Lawrence the man that the embarrassed silences started. "He seems to have won everybody over but himself," was one opinion. All agreed that he was like a flawed diamond. Many of the facets were brilliant, the others simply glass windows to a deeper self. He was a mixture of academic, man of action, romantic, and perpetual schoolboy. What would I make of him? asked C-----, his eyes fixing me in a steady gaze.

'What indeed? When was I going to meet him to be able to form an opinion? The snow was still pretty thick in the mountains but gone at GHQ.

'The next day D----- called me to his office. "Sorry about this, but I took the liberty of getting back to General Allenby yesterday when someone said he recognized you as someone else. It's all been cleared up now, I'm happy to say.

We can't be too careful you know. In that case, may I introduce you to Colonel Lawrence?"

'I stood up in surprise at D-----'s words. They were so sudden and unexpected. "A bit of snow does not stop an Oxford man getting through," said D----- signalling the door. I swivelled around and saw framed in the doorway a short, slight figure, barefoot, clad in white Arab robes. He seemed embarrassed to come forward. D----- left us. When he had, the figure stepped forward more resolutely and held out a surprisingly gnarled hand for me to shake. There was strength as well as reticence in the handshake. "Dr Watson, I presume?" he said smiling.

'"Forgive me," he continued. "I am the cause of you being shuttled from one person to another because I recognized you as Dr Watson, not as the name and rank that you are masquerading under. London is so secretive these days. There are no revolutionaries here, doctor, except ourselves of course."

'We both laughed and sat down. "Then there is no need to deceive you as to my mission, Colonel Lawrence?"

'"Indeed not. If London has sent you to keep an eye on me you may reassure them that I will carry out their deceptions for them to the best of my abilities, but I shall always champion the Arab cause."

'This man was obviously no fool and his rapid perceptions were just like Holmes's. I remarked so to him and he laughed a curious high-pitched laugh and said, "A compliment indeed. I thought you might think of me more as a Wiggins* than as a Holmes." We both laughed. The ice had been broken. He then decided that there was only one thing for it and that was that I should stay close to him for the rest of the campaign — '"Bull Pup' will be very useful,"' he assured me.

*Leader of Holmes's 'Baker Street Irregulars.'

'When I look back on that first meeting I cannot but reflect on how that first handshake seemed to sum up TE as far as I could judge. Strength and reticence. It had seemed as though he was hiding in his robes, his body shrinking from contact with the cloth and his face sheltering beneath the shade of the headdress. Yet it would have been impossible for him to hide, clad as he was in such contrast to our desert uniforms and the Arab's many colours. That first impression of a walking contradiction never left me, but as he stood there his brilliant eyes sparkling I felt that I was in the company of an exceptional presence only equalled in my experience by the great detective of Baker Street.

'The next few months saw us in action in many places blowing up bridges, and "planting tulips" as we called the gun cotton charges that we employed to disfigure the railway lines. I saw action by car and by camel. The movement of the camel I found very difficult to master and felt something akin to sea-sickness. "Bull Pup" certainly did his bit, usually as a support car. We even had a race on a flat piece of land and got up to sixty-seven miles an hour. Not bad with three-and-a-half tons of armour cladding on board, I thought. I enjoyed it all immensely. It was a soldier's life. Yet still I kept my watching brief on my subject. Curiously he seemed to welcome it as if he felt that he could not always trust himself to do his English duty and needed someone to keep an eye on him. He certainly led his Arabs with great gusto — almost too much gusto at times. He cut a splendid figure in his white robes leading his personal bodyguard of fierce fighters. The English military called them his cut-throats. TE retaliated by saying that at least they cut only the throats he ordered cut.

'I felt the years roll back from me as the mood of the hour took over myself too. It was as though I was making up for the time I had lost in my earlier campaign so soon cut short by that Jezai bullet.

'July and August saw an intensity of activity. These months were taken up in preparation for the final push to Damascus and the final overthrow of the Ottoman Empire.

' "The road to Damascus, doctor," TE once remarked to me. "Will we find enlightenment or disillusionment? Either way is suffering as Saul knew."

' "But Paul was his resurrection, TE," I replied.

'He smiled and galloped way ahead. After some mirage?

'One of our encounters with the Turkish cavalry had seen our three armoured cars destroy nearly sixty horses. Despite the jubilation around me I felt deeply saddened by the death of these beautiful Arab horses. Slaughtered by modern grey machinery, albeit Rolls-Royces, their deaths seemed to symbolize the death of the old order of which I was part.

'TE continued his constant travelling which I found very wearing. His abilities and energies astonished me and I feared that he would suffer the sort of reaction Holmes did after a glut of work before the final battle for Damascus. I travelled to the haunted old fortress of Azrak, to the port of Akaba which had been won so gloriously by TE, high-walled Itm, the other worldly Rumm and many other places besides. Sometimes I went by camel, sometimes in a Rolls-Royce armoured car, even by aeroplane for my one and only time. An experience that I was glad to have — but an occupation that I would gladly leave to others.

'We survived the flight and lived to fight another day, blowing up bridges and railway lines in an effort to cut Turkish communications and fool them into believing that the main push was to be in the east whereas Allenby was preparing his main strike force for the western coast.

'When we reached Bair and started watering our camels,

a long job at the best of times, but here the wells were deeper and so consequently the job took longer, I casually remarked to TE that it was Napoleon's birthday — one of the very few dates I could ever remember, history not being my strong suit, particularly chronology. To my surprise TE turned to me and replied, "Yes I know; it's mine too, I'm thirty today." He had a faraway look in his eye and I knew that he was in a very retrospective mood.

'"Shall we talk?" I asked him.

'"Later, perhaps, doctor," he replied distractedly.

'He spent most of the day in solitude, thinking. There was a squabble over camels which TE soon sorted out and we broke camp to meet up with the Camel Corps that evening. As fate would have it they missed the rendezvous and so TE and I were able to sit and watch the sunset with its brilliant, elemental ball of fire that gave one last blast of heat and light before leaving the wind-sculpted sand in silent stillness.

'"I don't want to see such a sunset at the moment," murmured TE. "I want the mist and cloud that covers England. Here the elements make for black and white, there the grey mists and clouds make for compromise. It has crossed my mind that the greatest single factor to influence history is climate. Thus the British see only shades of grey and so are ripe for conciliation and compromise, whereas the Arab has fire and temper."

'It was best to let TE think aloud; it was as though after so long speaking in Arabic that he could now articulate his thoughts in his own native tongue and the exercise was therapeutic.

'"The Balfour Declaration seems to be an interesting attempt at the giving of justice to a maligned race by an imperial power in recognition of the sins of another. I am sure that letting Jews into Palestine could be a good thing. The

Bedouin and other Arabs love their desert and their empty places; it is from such voids that they gain their strength, but to the Jew the town is all. They should complement each other — if they can forget being theological and be logical instead."

' "But who can predict the future? Has this war solved the world's problems? Does any war? Why did we go to war? I can't really remember now."

' "There is an Arab saying, doctor, to the effect that each man believes his ticks to be gazelles that can leap and soar, thus fulfilling their dreams. My ticks became gazelles at Akaba, and as we entered Jerusalem. They are firmly ticks again now and those that are not dead are eating into my carrion flesh like predators.

' "I have been in this part of the world on and off for the best part of seven years. It is too long this speaking in foreign tongues fighting another man's war.

' "Do you remember that flight from Guiveira? It was your first and only flight I believe, doctor. Did you know that I longed for the plane to crash so that I might be freed from my dishonoured life and my deceptions to this noble people? You're shivering, doctor, what is it?"

' "Nothing," I replied. "At least I hope not."

' "You wish to come into Damascus with us? Shall we enter in 'Bull Pup?'"

' "No, my mission is over. You must take my Rolls and the 'Blue Mist'. I do not deserve to be there. If you feel dishonoured by the work you have done in deceiving these Bedouin who are far nobler than I and many Englishmen believed before they met them, then you can imagine how I have felt these last few months having been sent to spy on you and ensure that you keep up the lie. If you had not seen through it all so immediately that day in D-----'s office, it would have been intolerable for me. Instead I feel that I have made a friend. I have been lucky, yet I fear that it will be many sunsets under moody English skies before your hurts are righted."

'TE seemed most affected by my words and sat cross-legged in silence. I noticed his toes kneading the still warm sand and his gaze intently studying the process. At length he spoke. "I now understand why Mr Sherlock Holmes so valued your company. You have the ability to listen and to give strength."

'"Holmes did not put it quite that way," I corrected him.

'"No matter, doctor, we all know what is meant."

'"You will be lionised in London. Will you accept the decorations of your king and the adulation of an empire?"

'"Don't ask me such a question. I cannot bear crowds, I detest being touched, and you know my views on receiving rewards for my mendacious work here."

'We sat in silence. The stars were shining and the earth smelled sweet. A tragic tenor aria welled up in my ears and caught the melancholy of the moment with cruel finality.

'"Just one question, doctor. Why were you known as Dr Ross to all the other fellows?"

'"Surely you realize the need for secrecy, TE."

'"I beg your pardon, I am not expressing myself clearly. Why Ross?"

'"I'll tell you when we meet again in London when all this is over."

'TE smiled and repeated the word "Ross" as though to remember it. He seemed content with some small crumb of comfort that I had given him. It was the last time that we spoke. The next day he was off on his road to Damascus and my job was done.

'Once again I was struck down by that curse of Empire, enteric fever, on my return journey. I only recovered enough to go out of my rooms here yesterday. I had thought of seeing my literary agent to sort out my book of Holmes's cases, but there was one person that I was burning to see before him — Mycroft Holmes. It was he who had appealed to my sense of patriotism and duty, who had suavely praised my abilities to handle TE, who had turned me into a traitor to conscience.

'I found him reading the late editions of the newspapers in one of the Diogenes Club's main rooms. As you may know, Stamford, no member is allowed to take any notice of any other one and talking is so frowned upon that three offences render the talker liable to expulsion. I was not a member and in no mood to observe such rules even if I had been. I forced my way past the porters and told Mycroft in no uncertain terms that I wished to see him — now! There was silent uproar among the other members and I felt hands on my arms and shoulders restraining me. Mycroft casually waved them aside and took me into the deserted committee room. As usual he was already fully cognizant of the reasons for my ill-humour.

'"You believe that I deluded you, doctor, when last we spoke in this room? Indeed I believe that I did in some way but only to achieve a greater end, the defeat of Britain's enemies."

'I was bursting with anger but Mycroft's soft voice seemed to soothe away the heat I felt.

'"You must think we Holmeses a poor set of brothers. We have now both deceived you. Sherlock at the Reichenbach Falls, and me in the committee room of the Diogenes Club. I can only plead as my brother did that too full a briefing might have led you to indiscretion."

'He stood before me head slightly bowed, his watery grey eyes peering at me damping down the fire that was still scorching me.

'"You knew about the Sykes-Picot Plan . . ."

'"Of course," he interrupted, "I drafted most of it."

'"And Mr Balfour's Declaration?"

'"Yes, I had a hand in that, I confess."

'"Were you not aware of the position in which you were placing Colonel Lawrence?"

'"I knew that some of his ideals would be slightly compromised by the more pressing affairs of war on a global scale. One man's delicate sensitivities were more than outweighed by the needs of His Majesty's Government and the peace of the world."

'"Then why not replace Lawrence instead of forcing him to live a lie which to him was like a living death?"

'"My dear doctor, you of course know the answer to that yourself, from your own observations in the desert. The Arabs would not have followed any other man by then. It was Lawrence or nothing, which in turn could have changed the war in Syria with the direst consequences for the British war effort. By keeping Colonel Lawrence on the road to Damascus you saved thousands of British lives. There are families who owe the safe return of their breadwinners to your efforts. You are an unsung hero, Dr Watson."

'"Yet I feel a heel," I hotly returned. "I will not be deflected by your praise from saying what I have come here to say to you, Mycroft."

'Mycroft simply shrugged and made himself comfortable in a large armchair. I remained standing fuelled by my righteous indignation.

'"Mycroft, you do not seem to understand the torture to which you have subjected Colonel Lawrence. It may be simply too great a sensitivity to you but to him it is everything. Granted that he knew about many of the so-called secret agreements, it still compromised him on a man-to-man basis with the Arabs."

'"Unfortunately, doctor, I cannot allow myself the luxury of man-to-man bases. I have to deal in Empires."

'"Empires that have been built by men like T.E. Lawrence. Not that he wants anything for himself apart from the right to be able to hold his head up and say that he has kept his word. An Englishman's word is his bond, after all. We are respected throughout the world for our honesty and integrity. Once we start dealing in secrets behind people's backs we lose our credibility and our empire. And, I regret to say Mycroft, it is those behind-the-scenes manipulators, of which you appear to be the prince, who will have the responsibility for that but I doubt that you will get the blame. After the disclosures of the Bolsheviks we are no better in the eyes of the world than the cynical French. Perhaps it is your French blood that has done this to you and you cannot help yourself. No matter what the reason, it is wrong and I blame you, Mycroft Holmes, even if no-one else ever does."

'By this time I was rather shaky on my feet but I still held my ground.

'"What has happened to honesty and chivalry?" I asked defiantly of the impassive bulk seated before me. His answer made me stumble to a chair in disbelief.

'"Neither commodity is deemed to be of value in the politics of the twentieth century, Dr Watson."

'"Not even by Her Majesty's Government?" I returned from my bemused state.

'"Whether it be Her or His Majesty, the British government must be as ruthless as its rivals, or sink. This is another world, Watson, it is time we took our leave of it before all our dreams are scattered."

'We sat in silence for several minutes. The clock chimed eight. "It is time for me to leave now, I am twenty minutes late already," prompted Mycroft. I felt terribly weary yet Mycroft made no move to leave.

' "I've been thinking recently," he broke the silence, "about writing a book on how to carry out government. I might call it *The Whole Art of Government* or some such title. One of the observations shall be that the greater the Empire the more fearful it becomes — in both senses of the word."

' "Another should be," I replied from some distant age or land, "now that we have entered into an age of machinery all loyalty to codes of conduct based on the 'cheval' are dead, and we are the poorer as a consequence."

'Mycroft nodded in agreement although he had probably thought of it himself many years before. He then asked me to dine with him at the Foreign Office, reminding me of the importance of the following day — today. He took my silence for assent and went off to telephone ahead. By the time he had returned I was in a cab hurrying towards this armchair.'

With that Watson winced terribly and clutched his shoulder again. 'I fear that the Jezail bullet has finally done for me, young Stamford.'

'Blood poisoning?'

'I fear so. The heat and the hardships of the desert, particularly the forced camel rides over rough terrain seem to have activated the bullet that I got in Afghanistan. Still I must not complain of an extra forty years of life after first being wounded in action.'

'And what years they have been, Watson.'

'Indeed. My years with Sherlock Holmes have made me the envy of a whole generation.'

'Only one, you think? You undervalue yourself and your friend.'

'You think so? Perhaps you're right. It will be twelve soon. Shall we have a toast to the new era — despite my misgivings?'

'Of course, but I think the toast should be to absent friends.'

At this Watson's face seemed to contort into a living masque of tragedy. I hurried to get the drinks, avoiding the gasogene in favour of its more modern counterpart. Yet another supercession of the machine age which would also become obsolete in its turn no doubt. Somewhere a clock struck twelve and I peered out of the window to try to catch a glimpse of the scenes of jubilation which had not abated all day.

As I looked Watson's voice entered my consciousness. 'I have an apology to make to you, young Stamford.'

'Oh, really,' I replied rather absently, 'I can't think why.' But before Watson could supply the answer or I could turn to face him I heard a sound that has frozen my blood from Alaska to Zanzibar. This time it was coming from an armchair in 221B Baker Street! It was the wheezing rattle of a dying man. I dropped the glasses and dashed to Watson's side. His head slumped forward and I heard just one word from his blue lips. It was not 'Holmes's or 'Stamford', or a plea to God for mercy. It was 'Mary'.

So died the man whom I had respected above all others. I now had work to do and a debt of honour to discharge. The briefcase seemed to call me to it. They could all wait to the next day. For now that most self-centred of emotions, grief, took over and I wept without restraint.

A Meeting with the Literary Agent

It was with very mixed emotions that several days later I went to see Dr Watson's literary agent, Dr Conan Doyle. On the one hand I was greatly excited to have in my hand Dr Watson's briefcase containing a set of stories which my old friend had worked on for publication after his war duties; stories whose contents were known only to the participants but, I felt sure, would soon be shared with so many admirers. On the other hand I wished that it was not me but my friend John H. Watson who was on the way to see his literary agent. I was a messenger of death and the role was not to my liking, particularly when I considered the identity of the deceased.

I soon found his office and quickly ascended the seventeen steps (coincidence?) to his door. A warm, brisk 'Come in' answered my slightly trepidatious knock. On entering I found Dr Conan Doyle reading a newspaper — it was the obituary page. He was marching up and down the room shaking his head murmuring, 'A sad loss, a sad loss.' He was a large, powerful-looking man of about sixty years. His face was large and open, coloured by many climates. His hair was streaked with white and his heavy moustache was almost pure white. The room was full of books and papers. Shelves were crammed with volumes on a vast variety of subjects from history to medicine, religion to mythology, travel to politics. Papers covered most flat surfaces, including the floor so that the Oriental rugs were like rich jewels covered in white samite. Not that the room was cluttered by them. There was a sense of order and discipline to it all, as though each pile of papers represented separate enterprises of either research or completed chapters of a new saga. There were various relics of palaeontology and archaeology which suggested a recent visitation of Professor Challenger, and on the walls hung photographs of sports teams and a pair of old boxing gloves: wherein reposed his tobacco, I conjectured.

'Do come in and make yourself comfortable,' he said, directing me to an armchair with his newspaper, and then realizing the impracticality of my sitting on it without crushing a host of papers he quickly apologized and swept them up with one swift movement of his strong left arm. I was seated, but Dr Conan Doyle remained standing, his heels balancing on the hearth edge.

'Can I presume you were reading my obituary notice of our lamented dear friend, Dr Watson?' I asked him.

'Indeed I was,' he replied. Then he paused and looked closely at me almost losing his balance and pitching forward into my lap. He then turned to the obituary again and quickly looked through it. 'Upon my word,' he said looking back at me. 'Stamford. Young Stamford. How you've changed, you're not as I imagined you at all.'

I let the 'How you've changed' pass — we had never met so how could I have changed, unless he had had a strong mental picture of me from Watson's brief mention of me? Another proof of Watson's talent, I felt like saying, but perhaps to all doctors young dressers need no further description. Let us hope that it is a happy characterization. I felt embarrassed about my sunken eyes and brown shrivelled look, a far cry from a rugby forward of healthier days. It was almost as though I had betrayed him by my subsequent existence in the Far East. I could not, feeling thus, return the doctor's frank stare, and looked to the briefcase and tried to say something about my reason for being here on such a sad day, but it only came out as a stammer. I stopped when I felt a powerful hand rest gently on my shoulder and a voice full of compassion say, 'Don't worry old chap, you'll beat it; Holmes did.' For a few moments my head remained bowed. What a third man this doctor would have made for Holmes and Watson. A scholar, a sportsman, a sage, an incarnation of manly virtues whose own exploits were worthy of the attention of a biographer of Watson's ability.

'Thank you,' I replied in a whisper as I fumbled to open the briefcase.

'To business,' he cried. 'What have you got there? That looks like Watson's writing.'

'Indeed it is, he gave these to me and asked me to show them to you. They are the last of a series that he was working on when he died. Some are complete but others only have an outline. He asked that you get them published as he felt that they showed not only Holmes's genius as a detective but also something of Holmes the man.'

By this time Dr Conan Doyle had taken the manuscript from me and was looking through it. 'I see what you mean. Presumably the *Problem of Thor Bridge* is complete as are some of the others, but the majority are only in outline with such references as "Holmes's humour is revealed here, exchange with Count Sylvius", and then a blank which we can only take to mean that John was going to fill in later when his time was not so pressed.'

Again he looked through the manuscript. 'Does Holmes know about Watson's intention to publish these cases?'

'Indeed he does,' I replied. 'He even knows about the unfinished nature of some of them.'

'Does he agree with their publication?'

'As you know, he never could agree with Watson's way of presenting the cases, and so he told me to go ahead and kindly not disturb him further as his researches were in a critical phase at the moment. Here I have his wire, it arrived a few days ago. He also has a few interesting suggestions to make about the cases in question.'

The doctor took the note, but before he started to read he asked me, 'What did he say of Watson's death? I am sure that the news will be hard on him.'

'Apart from suggesting that I write the obituary — nothing.'

'Nothing? This is indeed a mystery.'

'No, I think not, Dr Conan Doyle. You see they had already said goodbye when Von Bork was apprehended by them, and repetition would only be maudlin.'

'Or as Holmes would say, "work is the best way to combat sorrow". Hence no doubt his desire not to be disturbed in his researches. They have become more critical for the moment as his grief is greatest. His sorrow must be great.'

'As I think you will see from the conclusion of the case he entitles the *Three Garidebs*, Watson has let us know the true depth of Holmes's feelings for him. We can measure his grief despite the coldness of his letter.'

The doctor turned to the relevant passage in the manuscript. He nodded his agreement and then read Holmes's letter. When finished he closed the letter and appeared to be deep in thought. Decisively he looked up — 'Well, what do you say, young Stamford? Are you game?'

'Oh yes, of course,' I cried, 'but why not yourself?'

'Me?! The very idea. I'm only a literary agent who dabbles in history . . .'

'And whose interests and abilities go far beyond that. Beyond the grave even, may I say?'

'Have you not been inspired to that path yourself, Stamford?'

'I fear that my study of esoterica has been confined to too short and narrow a view.'

'Yes, many who find solace in drugs feel that they are crossing the threshold of infinity. It is only the truly inspired who see the falsity of this position. I do not mean that I am especially inspired, but Holmes is.'

'What do you mean, doctor?'

'During the hiatus he travelled far and wide in the East — as you yourself have done — but his travels were for different reasons from yours. I know you will take this in the right spirit judging from your earlier reaction, but your travels were primarily sensual despite the honesty and integrity of your original motives. Holmes travelled to learn more about the cosmos, both macro and micro. As you know he was only setting Watson a set of clues when they first met — as he probably did with you. You reacted differently so that we now talk of Holmes and Watson, not Holmes and Stamford as might have been the case in different circumstances. Watson's list of Holmes's learning was absurd in relation to his real knowledge. Theology had been his forte, and the study of the infinite was an inseparable part of his being from his earliest days. There were only two courses that his inquiries would lead him — Buddhism or Spiritualism. As you probably know he chose the former, I have followed the latter course.'

I pondered his words, as he paused before continuing. 'Holmes the man was different after the hiatus. He was more full. Gone were the youthful extremes noted by Watson. The machine, non-laughing logician was replaced by the philosopher. He had learnt to relax, a quality which earnest youth cannot experience, but the older Holmes was better for it. I hope he has found peace at last.'

I nodded my agreement.

'Now if you will excuse me, I would like to read the completed cases that you have brought me, and then perhaps we can return to Holmes's original proposition re their publication. I am a fast reader and shall not detain you long. Have a smoke if you wish,' he said holding out a boxing glove.

'Thank you, doctor. I wish to think, if I may.'

And so the two of us fell into silence, but not a listless silence as though on the banks of Lethe. We were both immersed in a far more turbulent river. He with the cases of the world's greatest detective, I with my memories and newly formed resolution. Cocaine would no longer be my aluminium crutch, I would be free of its influence. Holmes's example and Conan Doyle's friendship would be my spirit guides in this, my greatest trial.

The great man read on. At the end of *Thor Bridge* he nodded in recognition of a genuine masterpiece. *The Three Garidebs*, earned his grudging approval, as did the *Sussex Vampire*, but it was with the *Veiled Lodger* that he seemed most moved. He read over and over again 'The ways of fate are indeed hard to understand. If there is not some compensation hereafter, then the world is a cruel jest,' and 'Your life is not your own. Keep your hands off it.' Then in a lower voice he murmured, 'The example of patient suffering is in itself the most precious of all lessons to an impatient world.' He looked no further through the remaining outlines, apart from a very brief scan. He was in another world, where there is peace and there is snow. The Brahmin wheel was in a land of mist inside his inner thoughts. He was at one with Holmes. Abruptly he roused himself from his reveries and looked at me again. I raised my gaze expectantly but for a few moments he was silent, his mind working too quickly for the words to form on his tongue. Finally he said, 'Well what do you say to Holmes's suggestion?'

'I will if you will,' I replied. He looked taken aback for a moment, but his resolve would not be shaken. 'Then it is agreed, *The Problem of Thor Bridge*, *The Veiled Lodger*, *The Three Garidebs* and *The Sussex Vampire* shall be published as they stand. Which do you wish to work on?'

'Which do you wish to complete?' I replied, playing for time.

'If you insist, I have a liking for *The Illustrious Client*, *Shoscombe Old Place*, *The Lion's Mane*, and perhaps *The Retired Colourman*. I think that I could do something with them. What do you say, young Stamford?'

I had to smile at my perennial adjective — it was like a Christian name to me now. That left me *The Blanched Soldier*, *The Mazarin Stone*, *The Three Gables*, and *The Creeping Man*. Ideas were already forming in my mind. The first could be from Holmes's pen with an introduction to praise Watson's efforts and so vindicate his much criticized labours after all these years. I owed him that — as did Holmes, I felt. With the third I hoped to be able to act on Watson's directions and show Holmes engaging in witty repartee, as flashing as his singlestick. The fourth was a problem, but with *The Missing Three-Quarter* and *The Three Students* to guide me I felt confident of imitating Watson's tact and discretion re 'one of our great university towns'. That left *The Mazarin Stone*. For that I thought that I would try something completely different — a Holmes tale told in the third person, the only one of the entire published ouevre (if we discount the *Last Bow*). Carried away on a cloud of my own elation, I turned to the literary agent and cried, 'Agreed!'

Dr Conan Doyle chuckled deeply, and said, 'I thought that you would not be able to resist Holmes's idea. But I warn you I keep strict deadlines — there can be no indulging in habits that will fog your mind and blunt your pen. Is that clear?'

Despite the warmth of his face I could see that he was not making light of our enterprise. I rose and said, 'You have my word, Dr Conan Doyle.'

To which he replied, 'And you shall have my hand on it.'

We shook hands like old friends who had been lost but now were found. It was from that moment that I date my recovery from cocaine addiction for which I shall ever bless the example of Holmes, the memory of Watson, and the help of Dr Conan Doyle.

As we drank a toast in his office, Dr Conan Doyle spoke up with a mischievous smile. 'This will be a pretty puzzle for the scholars of the future. I wonder if any will spot our ruse?'

'It will take a bible scholar!' I remarked, unaware of the accuracy of my prophecy.* We both laughed. 'What shall we call it?' I asked.

'You mean when they are all collected together in one volume for publication?' he replied.

'Yes.'

'Did you not say that Watson had given you a book of cases? Surely the answer is obvious.'

---

*D. Martin Dakin was a bible scholar, who with others voiced suspicion concerning the authorship of the Casebook, although even he did not solve the problem completely.

I nodded my agreement. Thus *The Casebook* would be its title. We toasted that decision too.

So now you know the secret of the authorship of *The 'Casebook of Sherlock Holmes*. Some have suggested an alternative author for all twelve stories, others two authors (see the footnote on p. 53). In fact there were three. It is to be noted that those stories generally acknowledged to be the best of the set were by Watson, the next best by his literary agent, Dr Conan Doyle, and those generally agreed to be the poorest in the canon by myself.

How I cringe when I re-read *The Three Gables* in particular, with its poor portrait of Steve the negro boxer, and its less than sensitive dialogue between Holmes and Susan. This in turn reminds me of the so-called humorous exchange between Holmes and Count Sylvius in *The Mazarin Stone* which I had intended to be the verbal equivalent of Holmes's fencing and singlestick virtuosity. In my hand it has become a vaudeville routine. I can only say that as these were my first attempts at writing they reveal more enthusiasm than craft. What excuse can I offer concerning the inaccuracies of the topography of 221B in this same story? As you know I only visited 221B on the 11th November 1918 and on that occasion as you have also learnt, there were other things to preoccupy my mind apart from the layout of these famous rooms.

The Creeping Man appealed to me because of caprice — drugs and academics both subjects well within my purview.

Which brings us to *The Blanched Soldier* and the misleading data that has led many Holmesians to believe that Watson married more than once. I was telling the story from Holmes's point of view so that I could introduce it with some words of appreciation from Holmes as to Watson's work as a chronicler of the great detective's work. Holmes certainly owed Watson that after the many criticisms that he heaped on Watson's efforts over the years, and which the honest doctor faithfully recorded despite his hurt. Thus I had to explain why Holmes was without his Boswell. Only someone as close as a wife could have accounted for his leaving Holmes's side. Thus I have misled the House and apologize. Mary had died in 1893 I believe, and Watson certainly never did marry again. Watson spoke of how he knew Sussex well, perhaps Mary was buried there and on this occasion he was visiting his dead wife's last resting place.

I hope that these revelations do not dissuade you from reading the following adventures. You will find them of a very different kidney from these first efforts.

'Did Watson tell you what that important last medical case of his was?'

'No, I'm afraid not,' I remarked, 'but I felt as though he was leaving me clues. Whatever it was must have gone to the grave with him.'

'A great pity.' The mood had become more subdued. Dr Conan Doyle looked me in the eye and said, 'Young Stamford, I have an apology to make to you.' I looked up at him in confusion, a feeling of *déjà vu* disorientating me. These were the last words that Watson had spoken to me. 'When Dr Watson first brought *The Study in Scarlet* to me he could not get it published. I suggested a few changes. One of them was to cut you almost completely out of the narrative. The reason I suggested Watson did that to you was so that Holmes would appear to be even more of a mystery than he was and so engage the attention of the casual reader more readily. Thus instead of showing you as Holmes's good friend, we stressed his solitary nature and made it appear as though you only knew him through occasional meetings in the laboratory.'

'Yet in a way that was true,' I replied. 'That was how I

met him and it was where he told me about his cases as he worked on his experiments. I only rarely visited Montague Street and he was never in when I did.'

'There you would have met Mycroft, no doubt.'

'No, that was before my time. What a strange figure he was.'

'Indeed. I wonder what stories he could tell us all.'

'Perhaps he could throw light on Watson's last case.'

'I'm sure that he could, Stamford.'

It was time to go. I reached out for Watson's briefcase. Dr Conan Doyle passed it to me. For a moment we both held it and looked at the initials on the flap, JHW.

'I wonder what a Holmes could tell of the owner of this case. Sturdy, practical, with high standards of personal appearance, a military care for his equipment, and obviously a surgeon at one time in his career,' suggested Dr Conan Doyle.

'Why mention of a surgeon?' I asked. 'There is no indication of a doctor. There is no MD embossed anywhere.'

'True, but here where some stitching has been replaced it has been mended with surgeon's stitch. Watson must have done it himself on campaign somewhere.'

'But it is a new briefcase,' I said. 'Or at least relatively so. It should need no repair for many years yet.' Nonetheless there was the surgeon's stitch for all to see. About six inches of it, neatly executed but unmistakable.

Dr Conan Doyle rubbed his hand over the panel.

'There's something in here,' he said. We looked at each other, nervous of what to do next. 'Here, Stamford; Watson left it to you. It's yours to do with as you wish.'

In a moment my mind was made up. The two of us slit the stitching like surgeons in a field hospital with more casualties expected at any moment. I drew out two envelopes. Both were addressed to Dr John H. Ross, and both were handwritten. On turning them over we found that both had been opened, the seals having been broken. The seal on one was the House of Battenburg, the seal on the other was the Royal House of Romanoff. I nodded to Dr Conan Doyle and we read the contents. In a matter of minutes we had discovered Watson's last case.

Part Two

Watson's Last Case

Mycroft Remembered

Mycroft Holmes was Sherlock Holmes's brother and senior by seven years. Sherlock readily gave his brother the palm concerning deductive powers, a rare instance of intellectual humility on his part, but pointed out that it was Mycroft's physical inactivity that enabled the cadet brother to earn a living.

Physically, Mycroft was as rotund as his brother was slender and his eyes had a watery faraway look that the casual observer could misinterpret as the daydreaming that often succeeds a large meal and precedes a torpid sleep. This physical inactivity was a supremely efficient 'hide' from which Mycroft could observe those around him. Although described as an auditor of governmental accounts, Sherlock once revealed his brother's enormous influence when he described him in these words: 'There are times when he *is* the British Government.'

The adventure (as I am sure Dr Watson would have called it) which follows is one of those occasions when Mycroft Holmes was the British Government.

There is little more that I wish to reveal about how Mycroft came to communicate this adventure apart from saying that it was at a time when it looked as if ideology was becoming a slave to political opportunism and rational thinking was in danger of extinction.

Stamford

Mycroft Remembers:
The Diogenes

During the dark days of the Great War of 1914–18 my energies were greatly occupied by the problems of war and its governance on a global scale. Nothing quite like it had ever occurred before and as such there were few guidelines to use as reference by the administrators who had the awesome responsibility of waging a war of such enormous magnitude.

This I found stimulating on several levels. On one I could observe my fellow government officials and how they responded to this challenge. Some looked vainly for precedents to guide them and finding none either cracked under the pressure or found examples which they wished to believe could act as guidelines, so basing their decisions on the dubious foundations of ill-chosen, inappropriate 'lessons of history'. Needless to say, decisions based on such foundations were doomed to failure. However, others found inspiration in the lack of precedents and made up new rules as they went along. These freer, more decisive spirits often found themselves fighting a war not only with Germany and its allies but also with their more conventional colleagues in government. It is little wonder that the administration of the British war effort in those years has become a byword for inefficiency and ineptitude.

Another level was a more abstract one in which I could observe the problems of government without the human bit players. It was this study which inspired me to start to compile my thoughts which one day will become my magnum opus *The Whole Art of Government*. (I am sure that my brother Sherlock will appreciate the humour of the title.)

Much of my spare time was devoted to its compilation and many speculations filled my thoughts. As an abstraction what is a government's role? Obviously 'to govern'. But how much government should there be before it can be regarded as interfering in the rights of the individual? What is the best form of government? The one which suits a nation and makes that nation's people content. However, there are many nations and so theoretically many different types of government, which if appropriate to one nation might be anathema to its neighbour.

It was with a mind filled with such thoughts that I left for the Diogenes one evening early in 1916 at my usual hour (4.45 pm). Sherlock once spoke of the soothing atmosphere of the Diogenes. No doubt he was referring to the fact that apart from in the Strangers' Room no member is allowed to take any notice of any other one and that silence reigns supreme as a consequence. That might be true for him but after the facts and figures, lists and logistics of a day in Whitehall, my armchair in the Diogenes was the jetty from which I could sail the world in my mind's eye and turn my mind to the wider issues, their abstractions and resolutions.

As fate would have it I was not to see my armchair that evening for when I arrived at the Diogenes there was a note from my brother demanding my attention. As it was marked 'Most Urgent,' I foreswore my usual habit of going to my chair and only reading my post on my way home at twenty to eight. The note read as follows:

221B Baker Street
3.30 pm

My dear Mycroft,

Many apologies for such short notice but the Von Herling Ring is proving to be more difficult to crack than Altamont found in '14, thus I shall not be able to take on your next assignment for at least several months.

Need I say whom I appoint as my deputy? His qualities, specialities, talents and personal contacts with the subjects in question make him, I feel, more than just a mere substitute for myself.

Your humble brother,
Sherlock

I had no time to muse over my brother's use of the word 'humble' nor his choice of deputy for at that very moment he entered the club and extended his right hand to me.

'Mr Mycroft Holmes,' he said, a trifle formally, 'it has been too long since we last met.'

'Dr John H. Watson,' I replied echoing his formality, 'how good of you to come at such short notice.'

'You know me, Mycroft, ready in a moment when the game's afoot.'

You may regard me as a rather misanthropic sort but the good doctor's hearty, I may almost say colonial, conviviality frequently put me on edge. Often I had expected him to produce some sporting implement from his person and suggest that we play a round or a set or whatever it is that sporting types do in each other's company. However, as soon as the heartiness was penetrated there was the loyal, honest heart of oak which meant so much to my brother.

As we shook hands I could not help but think how well

Dr Watson looked. Thickset and powerful and with a good colour he appeared the epitome of the successful doctor. However, there were a few worrying signs. Instead of his usual handsome hunter he was wearing his brother's old watch with an equally tired chain. I was led to speculate whether his love of gambling and Beaune were having adverse effects on his pocket. Nonetheless the handshake was firm and there was eager anticipation in his eye and my uncharitable thoughts left me as I warmed to the company of this most personable of men.

We adjourned to the small chamber overlooking Pall Mall wherein we had first met. The doctor occupied himself with a whisky and soda as I withdrew various folders from the safe. Taking my seat I put the folders on the table between us.

'As my brother probably pointed out, he was due to meet me here for a short while to go over any final details before he took on his next case.'

'Indeed so, Mycroft,' returned my companion. 'That was why he suggested to me that I came to the club at twelve minutes to five so that you would have time to read his note before I arrived.'

'Yes, he would, wouldn't he,' I murmured to myself.

'He also said that I would be the perfect substitute for him on this case as it involves areas and people that I know,' Dr Watson continued, his enthusiasm unabated.

'Indeed it does, Dr Watson. In fact several of my colleagues suggested you as first choice anyway in front of my brother.'

At this Dr Watson blushed and fortified himself with another draught of whisky and soda.

'As you know, the powers of the Triple Alliance form a compact power group in central and southern Europe so that the forces of our Triple Entente are divided by land

and sea, rendering a truly concerted offensive almost impossible, communications being what they are.'

The good doctor nodded sagely at my brief exposition. 'However, there is one complication among all the others that I believe could be the most crucial of all. It is also the one that we know the least about and so are least prepared for. It was to be Sherlock's job to find out the exact nature of this complication and based on his judgement of the situation in conjunction with our projections he was to effect the appropriate response. That task now falls to you, Dr Watson. I must warn you that I believe that this is the most crucial imponderable of this conflict, whose correct resolution will decide the fates of at least three great empires, the course of this war, and quite possibly the history of the world for the next one hundred years.'

I was not given to dramatic statement in the way that my rather theatrical brother was, a point of which Dr Watson was fully cognizant, thus my words fully conveyed to him the gravity of the situation in my assessment.

'In these folders,' I went on, indicating the buff-coloured objects on the table between us, 'is a mass of information that I have been garnering for the last twenty years, but to complete them I need a man on the spot. You shall be that man, Dr Watson.'

He did not hesitate. 'Of course, Mycroft. Anything I can do to help.' He spoke as though it meant a trip on a train to nowhere more dangerous than Reigate. Little did he know.

'You are to penetrate the Eastern Front and then the inner court of the Romanoffs of Russia.' This time I admit that I was being a trifle dramatic, but Dr Watson responded magnificently — and unexpectedly.

'Of course, Mycroft,' he replied, again without hesitation. 'I look forward to meeting Tsar Nicholas and his delightful daughters again.'

I was somewhat surprised by this response and was eager to know more. Dr Watson was only too pleased to oblige. 'You do not know, of course, of the case I have called the *Adventure of the Illustrious Client.* It will be published after my death, but the illustrious client in question was our late King.'

This time is was the good doctor who paused for effect, but as it happened I already knew the details of the case from my brother and so remained impassive.

'As a consequence when I was in Cowes for the Regatta Week in '09 I was invited to join the Royal party and met Tsar Nicholas there. It was remarkable how alike he and George, then Prince of Wales, looked.'

'Many have noted the similarity,' I observed.

'The other occasion on which we met was in 1911 at the presentation of the prizes at the end of the Emperor's Rally for Automobiles. I drove a "Prince Henry" with my friend, Dick Renton.'

'The Dick Renton who recently died in Flanders?' I asked mildly.

'I am afraid so,' he replied with emotion.

'You knew him well, Dr Watson?'

'We first met in 1911 for the Russian Emperor's Rally. My original co-driver and mechanician had fallen ill and I was about to withdraw when he got in touch with me and said he would be honoured to help me out. The "Prince Henry" was Dick's as was a majority of the entry fee. He proved to be a wonderful companion and a very resourceful man. He even spoke fluent Russian. It is a sad loss that he has joined so many others in a Flanders field.' He seemed genuinely moved.

Little did Dr Watson know who Dick Renton was. He was a government agent, sent by me to help compile my files on Russia. I surreptitiously shuffled the file that was his work to the bottom of the pile lest Dr Watson should see it and suspect. The doctor's original co-driver had been a young, titled gentleman who had raced at Brooklands on several occasions but who had baulked at doing Renton's job. Not that he spoke Russian either. Thus he had a 'diplomatic' illness at the last moment which enabled Dick Renton to take over. It had been most convenient but the outcome was rather disappointing because he had not been able to get me everything I had wanted. I had not realized that Dr Watson had actually met the Tsar. As my brother said on several occasions, Watson was a man of great depth and wide limits. Perhaps if I had taken him into my confidence . . . Oh well, it was too late for that now and anyway he was about to be briefed for a momentous undertaking. I now understood my brother's reference to Dr Watson's 'contacts'. Perhaps he would succeed after all. One thing still puzzled me. 'I thought Dick Renton's co-driver was a John Ross, not a Dr Watson.'

Dr Watson chuckled to himself. 'Forgive me, but it is very rare for me to have one up on a Holmes. It is quite simple, Mycroft. Since publishing several of your brother's cases I have lived in the reflected glory of his brilliance and have found myself often pursued by members of the press. That is what happened in '07 when I wished to go on the Pekin-Paris Challenge. I did not want a repeat of that so I changed my name.'

'But why John Ross?' I asked, intrigued.

Once again Dr Watson laughed. 'It was simplicity itself. I simply opened the London telephone directory and stuck a pin into the page.'

'How elementary,' I remarked, somewhat coldly to judge from Dr Watson's rather nettled reaction. Even the most Byzantine turn of events can have a very straightforward explanation.

My manner became businesslike. 'Dr Watson, I must brief you for this case now. As you can see I have collected a great deal of information on the political situation but still something is missing, and I must confess that I am perplexed.

'Russia is one of our two most important allies against the Triple Alliance of Wilhelm II and I believe that she is in turmoil. I have been told that I am exaggerating by our man in Moscow, Buchanan, and he is a genuine expert in Russian affairs, but with all the respect due to him I think that I am right and he is wrong. Despite the fact that the nearest to Russia that I have been is my armchair in the Reading Room of this club.'

Watson lifted the decanter. 'May I have another drink?'

'I would prefer that you did not, Dr Watson.' The good doctor responded by returning the decanter to the Tantalus and merely topping up his glass from the soda syphon.

'As you know there are a great many dissident intellectuals exiled from Russia living in all parts of Europe. My reports tell me that although they predict the downfall of the Tsar, even the most fanatical seem to believe that this will not take place in their lifetimes as they once so fervently hoped and believed.

'The Russian aristocracy is even more complacent and believe that any uprisings by the peasants can be suppressed with ease and, if need be, severity.

'However, I am uneasy. There is some logic in my unease but mainly it is intuition — a faculty that I have not cared to cultivate but it has its uses.

'Firstly, Russia is at war with a sophisticated up-to-date mechanized state and after an initial run of success is now taking a beating. This has put increased pressure on her internal supply lines — supply lines which are antiquated and although internal are many times larger than the entire length of the rest of Europe. This has led to internal hardship, and I have found that people become more agitated over empty stomachs than fulsome rhetoric. Unless the food situation improves the Tsar is heading for disaster.'

'But surely,' interposed Dr Watson, 'the Russian people realize that in war sacrifices have to be made and the Tsar can appeal to their patriotism.'

'Normally I would agree with you, doctor,' I replied, 'but now there are further complications. Namely, the Empress, the Tsarevich, and the starets.'

'Can you please explain that, Mycroft?'

'The Empress Alexandra Fedorovna is in fact German and a first cousin to the Kaiser Wilhelm II, which makes her suspect in the eyes of every Russian from Grand Duke to serf. The starets is a supposed holy man who seems to be exercising uncertain influence over the Empress.'

'What do you mean, Holmes?' said Watson as though he was speaking to my brother.

'While the Tsar is at the Front the Empress is in executive command of government, yet instead of taking advice from the council of nobles or the duma, she prefers to be guided by this peasant holy man who knows nothing of politics. And make no mistake about it, his influence is great. All who have opposed him have fallen, from nurses to the Empress's own sister. It is generally believed that the Empress is undermining the war effort so that her cousin can defeat Russia. But what is the hold of this holy man over her? Surely not the liaison which is the gossip of St Petersburg despite the damning evidence to the contrary. In fact, so bitter is the anti-German feeling that St Petersburg has been renamed Petrograd.'

'And the Tsarevich? Surely he is only a boy.'

'Indeed he is, Dr Watson, but on his shoulders lie the

hopes of the Tsar. He is the Tsar's only son yet he is shrouded in mystery — and there I think is the centre of the problem.

'The Tsarevich Alexis is rarely seen in public and when he is he often looks pale and drawn. You may remember the *Daily Mail* published a long article on him several years ago saying that he had been attacked by anarchists who had thrown a bomb at him resulting in his severe injury.'

'That would account for him being pale and drawn in public,' Dr Watson remarked. 'He is no doubt worried about a repeat performance.'

'That is a possibility, doctor, and it would account for why he is often carried around by a sailor. Rumours in St Petersburg and Moscow suggest that Alexis is a mental deficient whose mental disabilities are reflected by his physical ones.'

'That again is possible. Royal houses throughout history have been littered with more than their share of lunatics,' Dr Watson observed.

'That is true, doctor, but my intuition and my deductions have made me follow a different course.' I continued, 'You may not remember our present King's uncle, Leopold, the youngest of Queen Victoria's sons.'

'Indeed I do,' replied Dr Watson. 'A charming, high-spirited young man whose early death was a great shock to us all.'

'Quite so. He died as a result of a fall in Cannes. He received a minor blow on the head and yet he suffered a brain haemorrhage.'

'It is not unknown, Mycroft. Some people seem to have weaker arteries than others, I'm afraid.'

'Once again this is true, doctor, but I believe that there is a killer stalking the royal families of Europe and its name is haemophilia.'

'The disease which prevents blood clotting and so brings about death by bleeding.'

'Exactly, Dr Watson. I knew that you would understand me.'

'Forgive me, Mycroft. I understand the disease but not your reasoning.'

'My agents in Prussia tell me that there is a mystery surrounding Princes Waldemar and Henry, and in Spain, Princes Alfonso and Gonzalo seem to be exhibiting characteristics very similar to the Tsarevich. For so many princes to be affected in such similar ways I feel that there must be more to it than royal madness.'

I paused for a moment and unconsciously took my brother's often observed pose of fingertips together, head back and legs crossed. Dr Watson had obviously seen the similarity and smiled.

'The heredity of the Holmeses,' he remarked.

'Quite so, Dr Watson,' I responded, 'heredity holds the key — of that I am sure. The common denominator to all these princes is that their mothers are direct descendants of Queen Victoria.'

Dr Watson spluttered on his soda. 'But Queen Victoria did not suffer from haemophilia, Mycroft. If she had she would have died giving birth and as far as I know all her births were quite straightforward.'

'What if the women were the carriers and the men the sufferers? That would explain it all.'

'But why haemophilia, Mycroft? Why not some sort of mental illness?' Dr Watson persisted.

'Alexis is not allowed to ride or hunt. The Spanish princes are dressed in padded suits and even the trees in the royal parks have padding on them. There are just too many coincidences for it not to be haemophilia.'

'It does not seem to be very sound reasoning to me, Mycroft,' my companion observed.

'I admit that it has elements of intuition in it,' I conceded, 'and it becomes more tenuous when we consider the role of the starets.'

'How so?' Watson asked taking out his pipe and putting it in his mouth but neglecting to light it. I offered him a Lucifer and pondered how appropriate it was to be holding an object so named while considering Gregory Efimovich the Dissolute, or Rasputin as it is rendered in the original Russian.

'You remember I mentioned the London *Daily Mail* earlier. The incident that it referred to took place at the Polish hunting lodge at Spala in 1912. Bulletins were officially posted each day as to the health of the Tsarevich, each succeeding one anticipating his death with the next. Suddenly he recovered and it is believed, in particular by the Empress Alexandra, that this Efimovich effected the cure although he was thousands of miles away in Siberia at the time.'

'How did he manage that?'

'I can only believe that he sent word somehow. By telegraph presumably; it is not only my brother who wires people all the time. However, the fact remains that since then Efimovich has become indispensable to the Russian royal family despite the opposition to him from other sectors of society.'

'But whether it is madness or haemophilia which affects the Tsarevich I know that Russia is in danger of collapse because of what is wrong with him. If Russia is in turmoil we lose an ally against Germany, and Russia is the last ally we can afford to lose. While Germany is fighting on two fronts we are safe, but if Russia withdraws we may well find that the Royal Navy is indeed all that stands between us and invasion.

'Thus your mission is to go to Russia and find out exactly what is happening. Your personal contacts should secure you the entrée to the Royal Family and your professional qualifications should make it possible for you to act accordingly and warn the Tsar of the danger of his position.

'However, I must advise you that I am in a minority of one and you might not find the Tsar receptive to my warnings. No matter — it must be done. I think if you talk to the Tsarevich's tutor, M. Galliard, you might well be able to get to the bottom of this mystery.'

With that I gave Dr Watson various of the files to read. First was my summary of how the Tsar was the most absolute monarch on earth and my observation of the more monolithic a power the more desperate is its opposition with a disinclination to compromise. Thus dissident opponents could be used against the Tsar by his enemies.

The second file Dr Watson obviously found rather heavy going as it was full of figures concerning Russia's economy. I précised it for him. 'What the figures mean, doctor, is that Russia has been undergoing an industrial revolution but instead of the success of our own, it has created much distress. There is now a large population of many millions who owe allegiance to no-one except their wage packets. These factory workers are a new phenomenon to Russia and they create many disruptions which not even Cossack whips can keep in check. Materialism is a dangerous philosophy with more heads than Hydra.'

The largest file contained the information concerning the Empress and the starets. Dr Watson read one of the letters, his face registering more and more shock as he continued.

'My God, Holmes,' he cried eventually almost bursting with fury, 'she has condemned herself with her own words if this letter is genuine. I can't believe it. She speaks to this Gregory in the most intimate terms. They must be lovers!'

'As you say, doctor, if genuine the letter that you are holding condemns her. I believe it is genuine.'

Once more Dr Watson almost exploded. I attempted to soothe him. 'On the other hand, the Empress always writes in such a fulsome style; such a style alone is not proof of a liaison, Dr Watson, as you well know from your own work with my brother in the distasteful realm of blackmail. At least one gentleman in Bohemia and several ladies of distinction have cause to be grateful for your sympathy in affairs of the heart.'

Despite colouring at my blandishments Dr Watson continued. 'But this is a peasant with dissolute habits, a known libertine if his nickname and these other reports are to be believed. Why, he has even been examined by church leaders and found wanting and attempts have been made on his life. This is all so different from our clergy.'

'Quite so, Dr Watson, and I am sure that I do not know the answer. However, I do know that the Empress genuinely believes him to have saved her son's life when the powers of orthodox medicine failed and as a consequence of that, if nothing else, she trusts him with the very force of destiny itself.'

Other files we worked through together for the sake of speed. On several occasions Dr Watson muttered that he knew several of the characters whose names appeared in the files. Sherlock was right: if anyone could persuade the Tsar of the danger that lurked in the bosom of his own palace it was Dr Watson. I busied myself with preparing letters of introduction for my emissary, although as it turned out he knew most of the people in question thus rendering my industry delightfully unnecessary. At twenty to eight we parted company. It was the last I was to see of him for nearly two years; in fact until he returned to the very room in which we were sitting to give me his report which I shall now use to reconstruct the events of Watson's Last Case, starting from Watson's point of view.

The Report

I

The Spring equinox of 1916 saw me boarding HMS *Torquay* en route for Murmansk. I had two identities — Dr John Ross and Dr John H. Watson. The weather lived up to its reputation for unsettled, blustery conditions which made the *Torquay* more like a buckboard of the Australian Outback than one of His Majesty's ships of the line.

The voyage was notable for the weather and the company. The bitingly cold wind, the silent ice floes forever changing colour as they silently slipped past us, sometimes giving us a glancing blow to add to our plunging progress, the accretion of ice on our superstructure which although, like the floes, was beautiful to behold but had to be hacked off lest it made the ship top-heavy and capsize her. All this was new to me having been used to sunnier skies when on campaign.

The company was no less strange to me as they were as disinclined as myself to reveal their identities or their reasons for being there. All that is except for one voluble American who claimed to be a newspaper reporter. No-one seemed to swallow that one, but his goatee beard gave him the appearance of 'Uncle Sam'.

The most unusual member of our party was an enormous

Negro who was said to be an Ethiopian eunuch. He seemed to find all speculation concerning him rather amusing as he always seemed to have a smile not far from his lips or a twinkle in his eye. I never heard him speak, he only nodded or bowed. The American reporter seemed to amuse him most of all as he tried to communicate with the mute giant by hand signals of his own devising and pidgin phrases such as 'Me, American. You, Ethiopian?'

This pantomime served as a distraction but I nonetheless observed my fellow travellers and pondered their missions, wondering if the gravity of theirs matched my own. Only one of my fellow travellers broke the mutual reticence of the wardroom and only then to observe that my tobacco reminded him of someone he once knew. My ears pricked up at this thinking that he was obviously one of Sherlock Holmes's clients. Alas no. It turned out that a hansom cabbie from his area had smoked a similar mixture and the aroma took him back to more leisured times, the power of smell proving to be a powerful if unregarded stimulus to memory.

The one man who spoke to me at any great length was the ship's surgeon. A powerful Scot named James Cambeuil who spoke in statements that suggested he was not used to being contradicted.

'You'll find the people poor and filthy and the nobles filthy rich,' was just one of his observations.

However, his theme was not an original one, it being shared by the rest of the population of Great Britain including myself, viz. the Tsar of all the Russias kept his people in cruel subjugation by force. It made my mission slightly distasteful to me that by helping the Tsar I would be sustaining a cruel tyranny, but the security of my own country was in jeopardy and that consideration overrode all others. On top of that what I had seen of the Tsar in Cowes in 1909 did not make me think of him as the ogre living off the blood of his people that popular imagination believed.

After three weeks we arrived in Murmansk, and were taken to St Petersburg by troika. I have rarely been more pleasantly surprised by such an initially unpromising proposition. Although a seasoned traveller I almost baulked at the idea of over 1,000 miles in an open sledge drawn by some very suspect-looking horses. None of them seemed to appreciate the company of the others and least of all the encumberance of a pile of wood, firs and humanity. It was my luck to be paired with the American reporter. He kept up a constant barrage of conversation throughout the whole trip despite the whiplashes of spray that the horses' hooves threw up in our faces and the equally sharp strokes of the wind. The runners thundered on the ice, filling my ears and drowning the words of my companion.

Despite all that I remember with awe the skill of the driver, the glow of the snow in the full moon and the amazing pyrotechnics of the Borealis.

In several short days I was entering the capital of the Tsar of All the Russias, St Petersburg. Its beautifully proportioned classical buildings were more like France or Italy than Russia. The sun shone brilliantly, bringing a glow to the scene so that all looked well with Russia.

This belief was strengthened by the British Ambassador, Sir George Buchanan, who begged to differ with Mycroft's intuitions. He stood with his back to the fire, reading my letters of introduction, the epitome of the career diplomatist, slightly stooped with greying hair that enhanced the air of distinction which accompanied his every movement.

Through Sir George I entered the social life of the capital, being presented to Grand Dukes and Duchesses and even several Princes. All spoke English and French with equal facility so that I was soon made welcome. The entertainments were dazzling with enormous banquets, precious wines, extravagant stories, exotic dancers, sensational singers, and tamed animals. If there was about to be a revolution, these people certainly seemed unaware of its imminence.

What of the people? I asked Sir George. 'They love their Tsar and call him father of the nation. Couple that with the power exerted over them by the Orthodox church and they are a people at peace — at least in the countryside.'

Before I could question him further the door to the reception room swung open and an expectant murmur passed through the guests. In strode a thin-faced, hollow-eyed man whose scrawny body was draped in a monk's habit. The guests stood aside as he purposefully traversed the room. He had the fiery look of the fanatic. 'Gregory Efimovich?' I enquired of Sir George, but before he could respond the monk had turned on me. Obviously he had not been pleased by me. His eyes bulged and the veins in his neck stood out as he volleyed a shrill tirade of Russian at me, his arms wildly flailing as if to emphasize his words. The other guests looked shocked by this outburst although I noticed one of the princes, Prince Felix, smiling broadly at the cameo being played out before him. Presumably 'holy' men were allowed such excesses in the drawing rooms of Russia, but it was time to stop this outburst. I turned to Prince Felix and asked as calmly as possible, 'Do you think that I could have a translation?'

The whole room erupted into laughter which did not improve the holy man's humour. He spat on the floor and ran from the room.

Prince Felix rose from his sofa, his movements languid despite the animation of his face, and held out his hand to me. 'Congratulations, doctor. You have managed to rid us of one of our less popular guests.' It was not until later that

Sir George revealed the joke to me. The monk was not Gregory Efimovich but his hated rival Iliodor who, it was rumoured, was writing a book in which he hoped to blacken the name of his rival and that of the Empress. He had not appreciated my error of identification.

By now we were back at the British Embassy enjoying a glass of crusted port before we retired for the evening. I urged Sir George to tell me more of the leading players in my case. He reflected for some moments, measuring his response in the way characteristic of all fine diplomatists. 'Russia is undergoing profound changes and those in the key positions are not suited to their roles.' With that he fell silent.

Thus it was that I spent the summer months trying to find out for myself. That there was unrest among the factory workers was undeniable and that food supplies were at best sporadic was equally undeniable, yet the people seemed happy with their Tsar if not their lot.

It was not long before I discovered that Russia was a land of rumour. Incidents which happened many miles away and in the utmost privacy would be the gossip of café society in St Petersburg within hours. This was possible because of the telephone and the secret police who seemed to be everywhere. One even followed me.

Prince Felix proved to be a charming host and we got on famously. As we sipped lemon tea from Lalique glasses he would answer my questions with a frankness I had not expected. He revealed that the Tsar was very popular but his wife, the Empress, was not. 'There are two reasons for this,' the prince said. 'The first is not her fault, but the second is that she allows herself to be used by that devil Rasputin.' At the mention of the name the prince became noticeably excitable and the spoon rattled in his cup as his hand quivered with emotion.

'Did you know, doctor, that everyone who has criticized that devil has fallen from favour? Even the Empress's own sister is shunned by her because she dared speak out against him. She is besotted with him. Poor Nicky. How I feel for him.' The langour had left the prince to be replaced by a steely quality that I would have thought him to have been incapable. 'Rasputin must be removed,' he said in a hoarse whisper, apparently oblivious of my presence.

'Are they lovers?' I asked boldly.

'Who knows for sure? He boasts that he has kissed the Empress in her daughters' rooms. He tells people that he can get them positions at court for certain considerations — and he does. He can only manage it through the Empress's patronage.'

Wherever I went the story was the same. The man Rasputin had bewitched the Empress and Russia was the loser. Yet nobody knew for certain what hold he had over her. The theories I will leave to your imagination.

Although the season was not in progress there were a great many people who had remained in the capital instead of joining the usual annual migration to the warmth of the Crimea. That seemed to be the only concession that Petrograd Society had made to the war.

Much to my surprise there were a great many English people in the city. They tended to be engineers on the railways and in the mines. There were several English clubs which could have been in Pall Mall except that the English newspapers were up to a month out of date.

One evening the surgeon from HMS *Torquay*, James Cambeuil, appeared and we chatted cordially enough. It turned out that he was a regular visitor and knew many of the members. Invariably our group was made up by Arthur Rowbotham, a railway engineer from Lancashire. A broad-shouldered man with thick brown/black brindled hair and an accent as broad as his shoulders, he was a convivial fellow who was in great contrast to his 'old pal', as he called him, James Cambeuil.

Cambeuil was on leave and having no family in England or Scotland he lived with the Rowbotham family in Petrograd. We all became good friends and I was able to enquire about conditions in Russia for the people.

'Not unlike Blackburn,' Rowbotham informed me. He did not elaborate — he was too interested in railway engines. 'There's hardly a one that works right int' whole of Russia, Dr Watson. Them's as do I drive me'sen.'

I was to be grateful for their friendship more than once in the months ahead.

Finally, at the end of the summer I was summoned to Tsarkoe Selo, 'the Tsar's Village', to meet the Russian royal family.

Situated a short distance from St Petersburg, Tsarkoe Selo consisted of the Imperial Park which contained two palaces, the Catherine and the Alexander, and outside the gates of the park a small village had grown up, rather squalid-looking in comparison with the exotic gardens of the Imperial Park and its graceful palaces.

The exact reason for my summons was unclear, to all intents and purposes it was purely social based on my letters of introduction and our previous slight acquaintance, but I could not help speculating if there was a deeper reason.

My carriage took me through the Imperial Park, past the proud Cossacks on their magnificent black horses and the company of foot soldiers on permanent guard. The doors to the palace were opened by two servants in crimson livery who took me to an ante-room where they handed me over to the next servants who wore a different garb. This whole process was repeated for each room and corridor that I passed through. Eventually I was met by a stooping old man with a fine drooping moustache and waist-length beard who held onto a long staff which was obviously for ceremonial purposes but was necessary for him to grasp for support. He introduced himself as Count Vladimir Fredericks, the seneschal of the Royal Court who would act as my guide to the royal presences. However, instead of leading me off to meet them he simply stood where he was as though in a catatonic trance. This was rather embarrassing but the moment passed and he looked back at me and said, 'Yes? Whom do I have the pleasure of addressing?' obviously forgetting the letters of introduction and invitation that were in his hand which had already explained my identity.

My next surprise was soon to follow. The doors behind the Court swung noiselessly open and there stood two enormous Negroes in gaudy uniforms of baggy silks, large white turbans held by gold clasps and equally white long curved pointed shoes.

'Behold, the Tsar's household, doctor,' beamed the larger of them. It was the silent Negro who had been on HMS *Torquay.* 'I thought we would meet again, Dr Watson. Your presence is urgently required.' His eyes were not laughing now.

We moved through the Tsar's chambers as fast as protocol would allow, the Count making sure that we observed the priorities. Instead of the gaudy orientalism that I had expected, the decor was just like an English country house. Before I could recover myself, the giant Negro was ushering me through a double door of linen-fold pattern, his solicitousness a veneer for his genuine concern.

'Dr Watson, the Tsar of All the Russias,' cried Count Vladimir, his voice cracking with intensity.

Was this the blood-drenched oppressor of peoples? The

tyrant who ruled by the knout, and the Cossacks' whip? His deep brown eyes brimmed with emotion as he held his hand to me. 'Thank you for coming so quickly, Dr Watson,' the warmth of his words matched by that of his handshake. 'Quickly.'

We hurried to the door on the far side of the study which was already being opened by the giant Negro, whose bow was not one of subservience but respect. In several moments we were in the ante-room of the bedroom of Tsarevich Alexis where five men stood, heads bowed, hands behind their backs. They stood to attention as the Tsar arrived. He waved a hand and they relaxed.

'Dr Botkin, Dr Derevenko, Dr Ostrogorsky, Dr Fedorova, Surgeon Rauchfuss — Dr John Hamish Watson of Baker Street,' announced the Tsar. We bowed to each other and Dr Botkin stepped forward to shake my hand — or so I thought. Instead he knelt and kissed it.

'Thank God that you have arrived. We knew that you were in Russia but could not hope to believe that it was true.'

Dr Botkin was interrupted by Dr Derevenko. 'Please, sir. You must help us. We are powerless. The Tsarevich is dying. You must save us all.'

I did not understand what his last words meant but was aware that there was a profound significance in them for them all. The doctors were desperate men. The Tsar simply looked at the doctor his eyes registering more in sadness than in conflict. He turned to me but looking to the parquet flooring as he considered his words. 'Were you aware that my son is very ill, Dr Watson?'

It was not time for disembling. 'Yes, sir,' I replied. 'That is why I am here.'

'In Tsarkoe Selo, or Russia?' he enquired. His perspicacity took my breath away.

'The latter, majesty,' I found myself replying boldly.

He nodded, and smiled to himself. 'Come.' We moved towards the sickroom door. 'Just Dr Watson, gentlemen.' My fellow medics looked to each other in exasperation expecting a lead from Dr Botkin who merely shrugged his shoulders in a gesture of impotence.

I shall never forget the scene as we entered the Tsarevich's room.

The curtains were drawn and the only light was from a multitude of candles, their flickerings catching on golden icons, giving the scene the appearance of a chapel limned by Rembrandt. Incense hung heavily in the atmosphere. The room was in complete contrast to the rest of the apartments, like a remnant of Russia contained in an island sea. It seemed to sum up Russia, that no matter how much the sophistication and European outlook of her rulers there was always Mother Russia at the heart of it all.

The large four-poster bed that contained the ailing prince was attended by his mother, the Tsaritsa Alexandra, a wraith of white lace and drawn features, her hair once red-gold was now liberally shot with silver grey. She rose as I entered, her face both regal yet imploring. Here she was not the proud German that I had heard cursed, but a distressed mother. I approached the Tsarevich to see for myself.

The Tsarevich, despite the warm glow of the candles, was ashen. His eyes were circled with heavy black rings and his lips were blue. Perspiration glistened on his forehead. At my approach his eyes widened, his breathing quickened, and he seemed to search my face. It was evident that he did not find what he was looking for, as he cried out in Russian and collapsed back onto his crumpled cushions.

I drew back the coverlets and saw the blood-gorged knee dark and distended against the sheets' silken whiteness.

'How did this happen?' I asked.

'He tripped on the stairs, doctor,' his mother replied.

It was obviously a case of haemophilia — Mycroft had been right on that point, but the youth was not in any condition to be tested as to his sanity.

When I gave my diagnosis the Empress shrugged in despair. 'We know what it is; we have our specialists. What we want to know is can you cure our son?'

There was no other answer but that the complaint was incurable. With this the Empress's expression became almost triumphant. 'So, not even the world-famous Dr Watson can cure my son. Are all the doctors happy now, Nicholas? There is only one who can cure him — Our Friend. Father Gregory.'

The Tsar silently nodded his assent. Out of the shadows stepped a powerful figure. Perhaps there was a secret door but whatever it was the effect was startling. His thick black hair was greasy with an irregular centre parting. His beard was long and tangled. He was of middle size and wore simple peasant homespun clothing which gave off a pungent agricultural aroma. Two things caught my attention — his hands and his eyes. His hands were long and well shaped but also manly. The effect was rather spoilt by the black dirt under the fingernails. By contrast nothing detracted from his eyes. Set close together they were dark and hypnotic and seemed to be looking straight through me. So this was the Dissolute One, Gregory Efimovich.

The Empress looked imploringly at the starets who bowed deferentially and approached the sick child. He raised his hand in benediction and murmured what I took to be a prayer. The child opened his eyes and smiled. Father Gregory looked at the Tsarevich, his eyes seeming to grow larger and more powerful. The Tsarevich's breathing grew more regular and he became calm. The starets spoke slowly in a very deep voice that was full of strength and to my ears, unused to the Russian tongue, kindness. Russia was indeed a land of mysteries. How was I to solve these riddles and act in accordance with Mycroft's directives? But the first enigma was, did Father Gregory have the ability to cure haemophilia, and it was to that that I turned my attention.

I observed this rough peasant bring about a miraculous transformation in the Tsarevich and his mother. Gone was the despair and the dread of a moment ago. Hope and serenity now filled them and acted as a magic balm.

After half an hour we all withdrew from the sick chamber, the starets returning to the mysterious void from which he had originally appeared but not before giving me a look of triumph and contempt. In that instant I determined my course of action. Tea was served. 'The biscuits are from England, Dr Watson,' observed the Empress.

'Yes, my cousin George knows that I like them,' added her husband.

Despite the civilities the atmosphere was tense. The Empress spoke first on the subject that filled our thoughts.

'Our friend is the only one who can help our beloved son, Dr Watson. Your journey has been wasted.'

The initiative was understandably the Empress's but there were questions that needed answers and duty that needed discharging.

'Might I ask how Father Gregory was able to help the Tsarevich when he was ill at Spela despite being many miles away?'

'He sent a telegram, doctor,' the Tsar informed me.

'What did it say?'

The Empress was quick to respond. 'Although I do not have it on my person I can remember the words quite clearly. "God has seen your tears and heard your prayers. Do not grieve. The Little One will not die. Do not allow the doctors to bother him too much." And the very next day the bleeding stopped. Alexis was saved.' Her face glowed at the memory of it all.

My next words had to be weighted carefully, but they were based on Mycroft's deductions and my own 'on the spot' observations. It was best to lead up to them slowly.

'What does Father Gregory say when he speaks to the Tsarevich, your Highness. Special prayers, perhaps?'

'Indeed the Holy Father does pray for our son, but he does that in his own chamber. When he sees Alexis he blesses him and then tells him Russian and Siberian folk tales.'

The last piece in the jigsaw was complete. How I wished at that moment that I was Sir George Buchanan with his great gifts of tact and diplomacy but it was no time for faint hearts.

'What do you wish to say, doctor?' the Tsar asked, his tone soft and encouraging, noting my hesitancy.

'Your Highness, I stand by what I said. The Tsarevich has haemophilia and haemophilia is incurable. Not even Father Gregory has cured him. He alleviates the disease's recurrences but he does not cure the Tsarevich.'

'He does far more than any doctor,' the Empress firmly interjected. Despite its large contribution to my recreation, gambling has never had a place in my medical ministrations but I gambled then as I faced the Empress.

'I will make the Tsarevich well again, your Highness.' My tone was determined and the Tsar responded immediately.

'What makes you so confident, Dr Watson?' he asked.

'Because I have seen through the starets.'

The Empress became so irritated that she dropped her teaspoon with a clatter into her saucer. 'So you too wish to denounce him.'

'No, your Highness. I wish to clarify his methods for

you. Having seen him and heard what you have said it is clear to me that he spoke sensibly when he advised you not to let the doctors disturb your son. Too much disturbance can cause the slowly forming clot to dissipate, thus prolonging the Tsarevich's agony. When he is afflicted he needs calm and quiet. The sight of too much worry and fussing will adversely affect his recovery.'

'But I have nursed him myself,' cried the mother within the Empress.

'With respect, that has been one of the problems, your Highness.'

'Explain,' she commanded coldly.

'Yes, doctor, you have insulted my wife,' added the Tsar, his voice hardening. The stakes were getting higher.

'Your distress has been conveyed to your son by your very presence thus causing him more anxiety. Anxiety is the greatest enemy to the afflicted haemophiliac. However, when you received the telegram from Father Gregory his words filled you with reassurance which acted through you to save your son.'

'That is true, Alicky,' the Tsar said. 'Don't you remember saying that you had lost all your anxiety when Father Gregory's cable arrived?'

The Empress grudgingly admitted that it was so. She turned to me. 'You have one week, Dr Watson. Save Alexis or leave Russia.'

The gauntlet was offered and accepted.

I went to work immediately. If my theories concerning Father Gregory's success in this case were correct, I was going to need allies. The five doctors obviously had no love for the starets and there was also M Gilliard whom Mycroft had mentioned to be contacted. On another level were two sailors who accompanied the Tsarevich wherever he went, keeping a watchful eye on their charge; these men also needed to be befriended. However, there were four allies whose loyalty and affection I believed could be relied upon. They were the Tsarevich's four sisters whom I had met as young girls at St Petersburg and Cowes several years before. My recollections pictured them as fresh-faced girls of great natural charm whose high spirits were only just held in check by their sense of duty and their love and respect for their parents. We renewed our acquaintance at teatime that afternoon.

As became clear, tea at four was something of a ritual for the Royal Family and the four Grand Duchesses would dress for it in white dresses. Although normally a family affair only, they requested my presence on that first day.

How they enlivened the atmosphere of gloom, although it was clear to even the most unobservant eye that they shared their parents' concern for the Tsarevich's health.

Now no longer girls, but young women, they were formally introduced to me by the old count. Olga, the eldest, had a wide clear face and the gravity that many older children have whereas Anastasia the youngest was obviously the mischievous one, her darting eyes and quick movements a constant reminder of her effervescence in marked contrast to the shy, placid nature of Olga. The two other sisters, Tatiana and Marie were contrasts in beauty. The one tall, decisive, self-assured, elegant, auburn-haired and grey-eyed; the other merry, outgoing, wholesome, and with eyes so large that they were called 'Marie's saucers'; their contrast was a delight. Yet the four were so devoted that they often signed themselves with the four initials of their names — OTMA.

It was the Tsar himself who helped us over the inevitable stiffness of the initial conversation.

'Which is your favourite case of Mr Sherlock Holmes, Anastasia?' he asked.

'*The Speckled Band*,' she replied instantly. 'It was so exciting. How did you manage to keep your nerve as you waited in the dark all that time, Dr Watson?'

The Empress remained aloof but she exchanged glances with her husband that revealed mixed emotions — hope, and the fear of daring to entertain such a thought.

Grand Duchess Tatiana asked perceptive questions about Holmes's methods, Grand Duchess Olga wished that the hound in the Baskerville case could have been taken alive, and Grand Duchess Marie wondered if she could have been as brave as Mrs Neville St Clair if her husband were to disappear in mysterious circumstances. Her sisters laughed and said that she spent too much time thinking of husbands and babies. However, the Empress brought an end to the levity when she observed, 'How I wish dear Alexis was here to share in our joy.'

The resulting silence was more awkward than the initial one that prefixed our reunion. Grand Duchess Olga held me in her steady gaze. 'You will save our brother, Dr Watson?'

The eyes of the entire family were on me. Perhaps I was intoxicated by the moment but I found myself replying, 'The Tsarevich will be walking in seven days, Grand Duchess Olga.'

The Empress was as humourless as a monolith. She would be counting every minute of those seven days and watching my every move, of that I was certain.

M Gilliard, the Swiss tutor, spoke warmly of the entire Royal Family. Of those whom I met he had recognized the humanity of them all despite the exalted nature of their position and the restrictions of their existence. He had also witnessed the Tsarevich develop from baby to adolescent and was more aware of the continuing tragedy of the

Romanoffs than anybody else, although incredibly he did not know the exact nature of the disease.

I told him of Mycroft's views. He shrugged his shoulders and threw up his hands. 'I don't know about politics or revolutions like your friend, Dr Watson. Russia is a land of whispers where a thought becomes a headline in hours — who knows what is the truth of it? But I do know that the Tsar and his family love Russia and her many peoples more than any revolutionary. I know that they have pledged their personal incomes to the war effort. Despite the wealth that surrounds them they are all penniless.'

Money was not a subject that a Swiss took lightly, so despite myself I was inclined to believe him. He was obviously devoted to the Royal Family and such devotion can be contagious but I had one unpleasant question to ask him.

'M Galliard, is the Tsarevich in any way mentally deficient?'

It was as though he had been struck a sharp blow. At first he was stunned but when he found his tongue the answer was emphatic. 'Mais non,' he stated. 'He speaks four languages, he is interested in all that goes on around him. Why, one day I found him in tears looking at the sky — he said it was too beautiful for words. If anything he is too intelligent to become a Tsar. He follows his father in more ways than one.'

Such fulsome praise was touching but it is always better to make up one's own mind.

The five doctors and surgeons gave me details of the treatment that they had been giving. All hated the Dissolute One as they called him. None of them knew Rasputin's secret but they agreed that he seemed to have brought about some remarkable results in the case of the Tsarevich. Dr Botkin bemoaned the fact that the Tsar and the

Empress would not allow them to use morphine to alleviate the Tsarevich's pain because they were afraid of the possibility of addiction. Whilst I could certainly sympathize with his attitude I could see such an instruction must have frustrated the doctors, but it did not explain Rasputin's success. He obviously had the fullest confidence of the Empress which was very important. As far as I could ascertain it was his eyes and his folk stories that held the key to the problem. Could it be that he had hypnotized the Empress and her sick child? His eyes were certainly powerful and it was possible that the Royal Family in their simple faith and desire for help had been deceived by a cunning manipulator of hopes. If this was so Father Gregory was certainly the despicable Rasputin of whom I had heard so much during the last few months. Could I compete with his eyes?

As to the folk stories, they seemed to lose something in translation when they were explained to me and I felt that the same would be true of British stories rendered into Russian. It was Grand Duchess Tatiana who came to my assistance. She advised me to tell her brother about the adventures of Sherlock Holmes. 'Although I would counsel you not to excite him too much — he might not be able to take the story of the Andaman Islander and his lethal blow pipe. At least not just yet.' The Grand Duchess Marie encouraged me with her kind smile. How she reminded me of my own dear wife at rest in a southern shire so far away from me now.

That evening the Tsarevich's agonies increased. His mother was at his side throughout, dabbing his forehead and kissing his glistening brow, but as each fresh spasm of pain overtook him he groaned ever more despairingly. Each sob threatened to destroy his mother's composure, but despite her obvious concern the Empress retained her aloofness towards myself. However, I detected a note of pleading when she enjoined me to help the Tsarevich. The Grand Duchess Marie slipped ahead of me and kissed her brother, whispering to him as she did so. The reaction was immediate. He looked up and his eyes widened like a child not in pain but as one who believes he has heard a sound in the chimney on the 24th of December.

'Dr Watson, Dr Watson,' he cried in a piping voice. 'Can you deduce what is wrong with me?'

I smiled. 'I have already, sir. You will be up in a week.'

At first he looked bemused and tried to lean forward. The effort proved too much and he slumped back onto his pillows, the perspiration standing out on his forehead in great sobbing droplets. The Empress gave me a withering look as she rushed towards her stricken child. It was then that I noticed standing in the shadows a look of triumphant cunning plastered on his face, the Dissolute One. I needed a miracle to save my position. It emanated from the deep pillows. 'Was the Lord Bellinger whom you describe in *The Adventure of the Second Stain* really Lord Gladstone?' The voice was a whisper but it was clear and controlled.

The Empress's countenance contorted in disbelief and the Grand Duchess Marie almost clapped with joy. As to Rasputin his eyes became as cold and as vile as a swamp adder's. I dismissed this vision of evil from my mind and sat next to the Tsarevich laying my hand on his forehead.

'There are many who would like to know the answer to that question, sir,' I confided.

'It is just that Lady Hilda reminded me of . . .' I raised my finger to my lips.

'Allow us our diplomatic secrets, sir.'

For the first time in many weeks there was laughter in the Alexander Palace at Tsarkoe Selo. The Empress turned to the starets. 'We have the adventures of Mr Sherlock

Holmes and your prayers to thank for this miracle, Father Gregory.' He bowed to his patroness, his face now a mixture of humility and simpering obsequiousness. The leopard had changed his spots but as our eyes met, despite their apparent openness, I felt that I was a prey being sized up for the kill.

For five days and nights I remained at the bedside of my charge with the Empress never far away. I felt the tension and lack of faith in my abilities fill the room like a cold vapour but when the atmosphere changed I knew that 'our friend' was not far away. Sometimes he would be lurking in the shadows, and at other times he would step forward and raise his hand in blessing over the child and murmur something in his deep voice.

These were not ideal conditions for my work but fortunately the rest of the family sympathized with me and the Tsar urged his wife to rest in the room next door. When she rested one of the Grand Duchesses would take over the vigil and the atmosphere became more relaxed and the Tsarevich more rested.

The pain that he was in was immense. His leg had been bent and held in a brace to accommodate the never ending seepage of blood. The joints suffered the most and any movement increased his pain but he bore it manfully. He even asked after my health and whether the Jezail bullet was causing me any discomfort. Such questions took his mind from his own distress, but it was the stories of Sherlock Holmes which took him farthest from his troubles.

On the fourth day I was roused from my fitful slumber on a sofa by the Grand Duchess Olga. I feared the worst and rushed over to my patient. He was lying stock still, his breathing not erratic as before but somehow excited. Something was not quite right. By his head lay a piece of paper folded in half. It had my name on it. The Grand Duchess handed it to me and I opened it to reveal a row of matchstick men. I was nonplussed but then I heard a snigger and saw the Tsarevich smile. 'I so enjoyed your story of *The Dancing Men* that I thought I would send you a message by them.' 'The tide has turned,' it read. And so it had.

By the end of the week the Tsarevich took a faltering step from his bed. The swellings at his joints had lost their anger and he was able to straighten his leg, and flex his toes. Sherlock Holmes had brought comfort to a frightened soul even though he was several thousand miles away. The starets led the family in prayers of thanksgiving. His continuing influence was all too clear.

At four o'clock that afternoon I was summoned to share tea and biscuits with the Royal Family, the Tsarevich sitting up in a divan. The atmosphere was in a complete contrast to that of six days earlier. The Tsar somehow seemed to divine my thoughts and observed, 'And on the seventh day will you rest, Dr Watson?' He was obviously a very perceptive man, a quality which I was about to rely on. As the family gathering drew to a close and M Galliard appeared to resume the children's lessons, I asked for an audience. The family was a little bemused by my sudden formality but I assured the children that they should be more concerned with their lessons than the words that I was about to address to their parents.

When I was alone with the Tsar and Tsaritsa I begged leave to speak frankly to them. A request which the Tsar granted willingly although his wife sensed a vague hostility.

'As I am sure that you are aware, Your Highnesses,' I began, 'I am in Russia not only as a doctor but as an agent for my government.'

'Your government, Dr Watson?' enquired the Tsar. 'Surely as an agent for Mr Mycroft Holmes.'

Once again his grasp of affairs astonished me.

'I would point out, Your Highness, that there are occasions when he *is* the British Government,' I replied somewhat pompously.

'I see, Dr Watson,' interjected the Tsaritsa. 'What is it you wish to say to us?'

'My mission was to find out the nature of your son's illness. Some speculation suggested lunacy, other injury in an anarchist attack. None knew of your son's true illness.'

'And so we want it to remain, Dr Watson,' the Tsaritsa pointed out. 'Not even M Gilliard knows exactly what the disease is, and of the doctors in Russia the five you met earlier know but are sworn to secrecy.'

'Only one person had an idea,' I replied, 'although he did not know.'

'Mycroft Holmes?' enquired the Tsar.

'Quite so, Your Highness,' I returned.

'And so one person guessed correctly, Dr Watson. What of it?' asked the Tsaritsa growing more uneasy.

'Mr Mycroft Holmes is the more brilliant brother of a truly remarkable man and everything he says is worthy of serious consideration. He fears that the more you retain the air of mystery around your son's condition the more danger there is of foolish speculation and even revolution.'

'Why should that concern you in England?' asked the now none too friendly lady.

'A revolution in Russia would be disastrous in our war with the Central Powers. I also know that your relatives in England fear for your safety and that of your family.'

'Thus you wish us to tell the world of the curse that lies in our House — brought by me, the German woman?' the Empress hissed. 'Do you think that would stop a revolution? It would be an invitation to every anarchist, revolutionary, and crack-pot to try to kill my son. No, I will not allow it!'

'If not that, then at least dispense with the services of Father Gregory,' I suggested. 'I have shown that your son's recovery does not depend on him alone and he brings disrepute on your House.'

For the first time since I had met her the Empress's face coloured. 'That is unthinkable, Dr Watson.'

'Forgive me, Your Highness, but would it not be better to give details of your son's condition and remove the cause of ill-informed intrigue and gossip? Once the people know of the Tsarevich's complaint you will have sympathy from your people, not hostility,' I entreated.

'You have been given the reasons for our decision,' the Empress said in cold, clear tones that brooked no shading.

The Tsar sat by her, his eyes sad but his jaw set.

My mission had failed.

The British Embassy did not prove a happy haven of return. The news from the Front went from bad to worse. The mud of the Somme seemed to be obscenely swallowing the life blood of a generation in cruel mockery of the once great victory of Agincourt fought five hundred years before on the same ground.

My reports made, there was only one thing to do — return to London. It was then that a new turn of events ensured that I had not seen the last of Mother Russia.

The day after my return to the British Embassy in Petrograd as I should call St Petersburg, I received a note as I sat down for breakfast. It read 'From one enthusiast to another'. Obeying Sir George's summons I went outside and there before me was a gleaming Rolls-Royce. 'From the Tsar if I am not mistaken, Dr Watson,' Sir George said as we went to inspect my gift. 'See the Romanoff eagle on the steering boss.'

Obviously my exertions of the previous seven days and

the chill from driving in the crisp Baltic air had proved too much for me. I fell ill with a fever that would have become double pneumonia but for Dr Cambeuil's ministrations. It was two months before I was able to take an interest in the world outside, but what news there was. Tsar Nicholas had returned to the Front and the Empress had been ruling in his stead, aided by Father Gregory. Every layer of society was now open in its criticism of the Romanoff regime. Mycroft's predictions were becoming truer every day.

My first encounter with a mirror shocked me. I was drawn and haggard and my beard had grown. 'I should keep that if I were you,' observed Cambeuil. 'That is if you intend to keep driving that car of yours, not that you'll ever see me in one. Infernal combustion engine is what it is.'

The advice proved sapient, the prediction oblique.

Several weeks later my health was sufficiently regained for me to attend the ballet. A box was provided by Duchess Prushnikov to watch Mathulde Kschessinka, the prima ballerina assoluta of the Imperial Ballet, dance the 'Pharaoh's Daughter'. The Season was in full swing and it looked as though there was no war anywhere. The fact that over one million Russians had died in the summer offensive was a matter of complete indifference to Society.

At supper that evening the reason for my invitation became clear. As we reclined on opulent tapestry couches drinking chilled vodka, steaming tea, or bubbling hot chocolate, the Duchess Prushnikov asked me bluntly, 'Do you believe that there is going to be a revolution in Russia, doctor?'

My response was equally candid, 'If certain things are not righted — yes, Duchess.'

'Good. Then you will join us in getting rid of Nicky and replacing him with Alexei.'

Sir George and I made our excuses and left.

'We must warn them,' I urged on entering the embassy.

'By all means, but they probably know already. The police are effective sentinels and the Duchess is hardly discreet,' he replied.

'But surely...'

'Have no fear, Dr Watson,' he suavely assured me, 'the Tsar will be kept informed and will note that another volatile reagent has just let off steam. Rather that than the silent ones who store up hatreds. It is the Slavic way.'

Despite the absolute confidence of Sir George's words I wired the Royal Family offering them my services. There was no reply. The Tsar was in Kiev and the Empress was alone, advised by Rasputin.

At the beginning of December I was to see Rasputin and Slavic steam release again in one evil cocktail.

I had arranged to meet James Cambeuil and Arthur Rowbotham at the Yar restaurant. It was a popular spot and consequently very crowded. The Yar was a large building with a music hall, balconies, private chambers, and public rooms. It was always very merry, and shrieks and whistles often rent the air but on this occasion it was the cry of a wild animal, a bull in temper that filled the air and silenced the multitude. As everyone stood as still as a photograph, the unmistakable figure of Rasputin smashed out of one of the private booths. Women screamed, glass shattered spraying crystal colours and astragals, furniture was thrown aside. Even those in the upper balconies fell silent and lent over to witness the spectacle. He was obviously very drunk. Spittle ran from his lips and mingled with debris already caught up in his matted beard. His clothes, now silks not peasant homespun, were torn and his steps unsteady.

The people who had but a moment ago been a carefree audience of the music hall performance now shrank in fear and loathing from this beast in human form and as they retreated a space opened up between Rasputin and myself. When he caught sight of me he stopped staggering and roaring. Instead he fixed his eyes on me and approached me on slow unsteady legs, the sound of his boots clearly audible on the polished wooden floor in that sea of frightened silence. His eyes were the distillation of evil: it was as though he was a cobra coil sprung to strike and I was his target. I stood my ground and became aware of Cambeuil and Rowbotham standing at my shoulders. The Holy Father spat on the floor and then began to chant, 'Doctor, Doctor.' After that performance he boomed with laughter and ran at me. Before he had gone three paces he slipped and a group of policemen caught hold of him and dragged him from the premises cursing, kicking and spitting.

Uproar returned but above it all a young man jumped onto a table and cried, 'Who has the courage to save us from this beast? Revolution threatens and an obscure starets must govern Russia no longer.' The crowd cheered its approval but none moved to carry out the entreaty.

'Words, only words,' grumbled Cambeuil.

'Aye,' agreed Rowbotham.

As they spoke I noticed the door to one of the more exclusive rooms swing open. Inside was Prince Felix, white and trembling with emotion.

January 1st 1917 was a bright sunny day. There had been some heavy snowfalls in the night and the Neva was largely ice but the clear blue sky welcomed the new year with a smile. Petrograd once more had been alive with rumours. Where was Rasputin? Three days before he had been seen getting into Prince Felix's motor car to go to a late night party, and he had not returned. By mid-afternoon people were hugging each other in the street saying, 'The beast is dead. Rasputin is no more. Long live the Tsar. We have our Tsar back.'

The report of Rasputin's end was as spectacular as his life. Prince Felix had lured him to a cellar and with the help of several accomplices had proceeded to poison, beat, shoot and finally drown the Dissolute One.

The next day a cable arrived for me as I packed. 'Stay until further notice. Mycroft Holmes.' This was a puzzling order as the greatest obstruction to civil order was now removed. Even Sir George Buchanan's sensitive political antennae could not pick up the reason for concern, but Mycroft, I knew, did not say things lightly.

Several weeks later I was in the English Club with James Cambeuil and Arthur Rowbotham. Between sips of his Imperial Russia stout Rowbotham confided that things were going from bad to worse with the trains. 'If they don't sort it out, there'll be no food in Petrograd in a couple of weeks.'

'I shall be away by then, thank Heaven,' responded Cambeuil looking through the single malt in his crystal glass as though contemplating the future. 'And yourself, doctor?' he enquired of me. 'You're still under orders, I trust?'

Before I could answer, one of the club stewards rushed into the bar and cried, 'There's rioting all over the city. There's no food in the last train.'

'Just as ye said, Arthur,' observed Cambeuil without changing his position. 'Except you got your timing wrong. A poor habit for a train driver, I'll be bound.'

Arthur Rowbotham became agitated. 'Excuse me, gents, but I'd best be off, have to see the wife. She is still not used to Cossacks whipping people in't street.'

'I'll come with ye,' volunteered Cambeuil and they left quickly. Despite his almost casual air, James Cambeuil was obviously worried — he did not finish his drink before leaving.

How to write of such momentous events which witnessed the fall of a three hundred year old dynasty and replace it with a godless ideology? As far as I can judge the main episodes were as follows: there was a lack of food which led to the people of Petrograd rioting. Troops were brought in but instead of quelling the disturbances they joined it. Even the Tsar's personal bodyguard at Tsarkoe Selo, who had sworn allegiance to him personally, also defected. Tsar Nicholas II saw that to continue would bring civil war on Russia. Thus he abdicated, but not in favour of his son but his younger brother, Michael. It was this one act that stunned observers. Why deprive the Tsarevich of his right? was the question on everyone's lips. The reason was of course that the Tsar knew he would be exiled and his son ruled by others at least until his age of majority. Even if he survived that he was still at the mercy of a sudden fall or injury. How could he survive among unsympathetic strangers ruling such a vast empire? In the end it was his family that was empire enough for the last anointed Romanoff Tsar of all the Russias.

The signing of the abdication took place on a train near Pskov and the Tsar was later reunited with his family in Tsarkoe Selo where they were able to be kept as prisoners until the new Duma or Parliament could decide what to do with them.

The community of the ex-Tsar's family and retainers remained at Tsarkoe Selo for several months. All communications were censored. At all times armed guards surrounded what remained of the household. What had become of them? Rumours persisted of course. Newspapers were full of 'revolutions' of Rasputin and the Empress. The Tsar was shown laughing and eating a large meal while political prisoners were done to death and Russian peasants starved before his eyes. My blood boiled at this misrepresentation but what could I do?

Diplomatic activity in the Embassy was intense with telegrams passing between Petrograd and London every single day. Athough I was a government agent, Sir George did not allow me to read any of them. Finally, a message arrived for me from Mycroft Holmes. It purported to be a detailed criticism of my report; in fact it was a code which explained the position. It made grave reading.

The King had wanted to do everything in his power to assist the escape of the Royal Family but had been over-ruled by the Prime Minister who regarded the overthrow of the Romanoffs as a step in the right direction in the progress of man. In the face of this the King did not insist. At least not to the Prime Minister. Instead he referred to Mycroft Holmes, who in turn referred to me. Money was to be made available for whatever scheme I could devise, but as Mycroft pointed out I was on the spot and all final decisions were mine.

This was a weighty task indeed. What would Holmes have done in my place? A series of audacious enterprises, bewildering disguises and a final 'coup de theatre' no doubt. But what did I have? Funds, a Rolls-Royce, only a smatter-ing of Russian taught to me by the Tsarevich, and a phy-sique still weak and wasted from its trials. Then there was Cambeuil, Rowbotham and the Tsar's household, but what could I make of them?

I looked at a map of Russia. Escape by railway to Murmansk and a British ship was the obvious route — so obvious that others would be waiting to intercept us. The Crimea was friendly but could only be reached by rail through some of the most violently anti-Tsarist towns and country in Russia. Having discarded the impossible what remained was improbable but possible. My idea was to take the family to freedom via Japan. In other words travel the entire length of Asiatic Russia thus leaving the revolution-ary lands of the European in Russia to look to themselves.

It was a very long shot and I smoked several pipes over it, but I could think of no alternative. With Rowbotham driving the train and Cambeuil lending a hand as well as the Royal Family's retainers, there was a chance of success.

When they were approached, Cambeuil and Rowbotham readily agreed to help but Rowbotham pointed out that we must avoid Yekaterinberg at all costs because the people there were steelworkers or miners who hated the Tsar more than anyone else in the world.

There remained one great difficulty. How could the Royal Family, its suite, and a complete train be spirited away from Tsarkoe Selo?

The canny Cambeuil listened to my exposition and sug-gested, 'If ye have funds why not bribe the guards?'

From what I knew of the revolutionary leaders the guards would be forfeiting their lives if they allowed their charges to escape. 'In that case, man,' persisted the little Scot with all the tenacity of his race, 'ransom them from the revolu-tionaries. That way it's all above board.'

The idea was an attractive one. If made through the correct channels it must surely work. Consultations with Sir George did much to dampen my spirits. He communicated with London but found that attitudes had hardened. The British people, steeped in the belief that the Tsar was a blood-soaked autocrat, would not have him in England. This in turn had made both Government and Monarch not wish to risk unpopularity. Officially the funds were stopped. My telegrams to Mycroft went unanswered. The position was hopeless.

There is much truth in old proverbs, the accumulated wisdom of the countless generations, as was proved to me the next day. It was my darkest hour. I felt that I had betrayed all the trust that had been put in me by both

Sherlock and Mycroft Holmes, the Tsar, OTMA and the Tsarevich.

When the final telegram from London had arrived which withdrew any offer of asylum from the British Government, even Sir George had broken down and begged me to save the Romanoffs and the honour of our country. The burden of responsibility was intolerable and my health began to suffer. But dawn came in the shape of a small round man with dark thinning hair, sleepy spaniel eyes, and the general air of a mammal approaching hibernation. However, on seeing me he was startled to exclaim, 'It's impossible. You look nothing like Dr Watson.' Sir George re-affirmed my identity.

'*The Strand* has been too complimentary, I fear,' I observed.

'No, sir, not that,' he replied excitedly turning to Sir George. 'It's almost uncanny.'

'What are you talking about, sir?' I exclaimed.

'Allow me to introduce Mr Sidney Gibbs, the Tsarevich's English tutor,' said the diplomatist with a bow.

We exchanged a long look and nodded to each other. An idea had sprung up with the need of words. We both turned to Sir George. He too was thoughtfully nodding. 'Dr Watson, Mr Sidney Gibbs, English tutor to the Tsarevich and at present one of the few people who has seen the Tsar in the last few days. We can trust his eye.'

'I think we have some details to thrash out, don't you, gentlemen?' he said, the lassitude in his eyes replaced by a burning energy.

II

An hour later a Rolls-Royce emerged from the British Embassy at Petrograd. Instead of a Romanoff eagle on the steering boss there was a brass Union flag. Two other

Union flags fluttered on the bonnet as the car, driven by a chauffeur in riding helmet, goggles, driving mask, fur coat and gauntlets and conveying the Tsarevich's tutor and an eminent Scottish naval surgeon, made its way south on the Tsarkoe Selo road.

Petrograd was ominously quiet. Workers in heavy boots and rough woollen overcoats, peasants in felt boots and coloured padded coats paused to observe its passing. Headscarves flapped in the breeze but their wearers registered no emotion and soon returned to their previous occupations. For the moment they were spent.

As the car drew nearer to Tsarkoe Selo, guards with red armbands began to fill the road. The gates were heavily guarded but when Mr Gibbs spoke up the party was allowed to pass unhindered. Some of the soldiers had the slit eyes and humourless lupine faces of the Asiatic of the Steppes, others the heavy frames and blotchy faces of ex-factory workers. The revolution obviously appealed to more than one race or group.

The car drew up to the steps of the Alexander palace and the small party disembarked. The guards, at first surly, became more respectful when Mr Gibbs addressed them and they saw the flags on the car. Now instead of an absent-minded old Finnish Count with a long beard and moustache, supported by an army of brightly liveried servants there was an army of ex-servants and former factory workers with red armbands, most of whom looked a disgrace to any regiment except one of successful revolutionaries.

The chauffeur looked at his watch. Four o'clock — tea time. The party was directed to the office of the acting commander Colonel Eugene Kobylinsky. He was an imposing figure who walked with a slight limp and he observed something similar in the carriage of the chauffeur. Although only recently installed as commander this twice-wounded veteran of the Eastern Front had done much to shelter the Royal Family from the rude soldiery of their captors. He was a soldier not a politician. He saluted Mr Sidney Gibbs and, when he was introduced, Surgeon James Cambeuil. The chauffeur remained anonymous.

'You will hurt the Tsarevich, not help him, with all these doctors, Mr Gibbs,' he said warmly. Neither surgeon nor chauffeur understood the Russian's words.

Mr Gibbs waited until the guards had closed the doors before he introduced the newcomers. 'Surgeon James Cambeuil of the British Navy,' he intoned. The Tsar bowed and the Tsarevich's companion, the sailor Nagorny, saluted. 'And may I present our chauffeur . . .' the tutor continued but putting a finger to his lips and urging silence with a downward gesture of his palm. 'Tsar Nicholas II of All the Russias.'

The chauffeur removed his helmet, goggles, scarf and driving mask to reveal the double of the displaced monarch. The entire royal retinue let out a gasp except for the Tsar himself who stepped forward and said, 'Dr Watson, I assumed you had returned to Baker Street.' Despite all his self-discipline his eyes brimmed and he hugged the famous biographer with passion. Even the Tsaritsa was overcome with emotion and clasped his hand warmly, but she already sensed danger.

'Your Highness, I am honoured to be in your presence again, and able to repeat my offer of assistance,' the doctor replied. The Tsaritsa blushed at the reference to the unanswered telegram. 'We have so little time, sir. We must swop clothes now. You know you can trust me.'

The Tsar and his wife exchanged glances. 'But I cannot leave my family, doctor. The Colonel Kobylinsky is our friend, as is the Premier Kerensky, so we have nothing to fear. We will soon be saved by our British cousins.'

The doctor's face grew grim. From within the lining of his gauntlets he withdrew several telegrams, all originating from London. The Tsar's face became ashen, as did the Tsaritsa's when they read them. Mr Gibbs outlined the plan as quickly as he could while Cambeuil and Nagorny stood by the door to prevent intrusion. The substitution was effected in a few minutes. Several moments later the door burst open and a group of unshaven soldiers appeared at the door.

'There they are. The blood-drinking Romanoffs,' they cried. One approached Watson as though to strike him but the 'Tsar' stood proudly and the soldier slunk back muttering oaths as he did so. The others followed him from the room.

'Well done, doctor,' said the tutor. 'He will think twice before approaching you again. I must now help the surgeon to examine the Tsarevich otherwise our mission will be suspected.'

'There is one question that I wish to ask,' the Tsar interjected. 'Am I to believe that I have taken over the role of chauffeur?'

'Yes, Your Highness,' replied Gibbs breezily.

'Then we must prepare ourselves for a shock,' continued the Tsar. 'I have never driven a Rolls-Royce in my life.'

The three Britons gasped.

'But Your Highness,' stammered Watson, 'I thought you to be an enthusiast. The note . . .'

'Indeed, doctor, I am an enthusiast, not a driver. The note and the car were from the Empress.'

It was Dr Watson's turn to blush but no amount of colouring could obscure the problem. Before anyone's resolve could sag further Dr Watson stepped in. 'In that case I shall explain while Gibbs and Cambeuil go about their business.'

The next few minutes were spent in feverish activity with Dr Watson explaining the intricacies of crank handles, advance-retards, clutches, gear changes, throttles, revs and brakes. The Tsar listened intently, well aware that the slightest mistake could lead to the discovery of the deception and dire consequences.

'First you see Surgeon Cambeuil to his seat,' the doctor instructed. 'Next ensure that the gears are in neutral. I left them in first when I parked, so you must release them. The gear lever is the larger of the two levers outside the car which you release by gripping the handle and ratchet lever then moving the whole stick to the left. Next you prime the petrol, then you must turn the crank handle over. Do not forget to keep your thumb and fingers on the same side of the handle. It is located at the front of the car and it is that which starts the engine. You get into the car via the passenger door and slide across the seat. To move off, you must engage first gear. This is done by depressing the clutch which is the pedal on the floor to the left. Then you move the gear lever to the right. Next release the hand brake which is next to the gear lever. Finally let the clutch pedal up and depress the accelerator. Try not to use the foot brake as it works off the transmission and is only intended for emergency use.'

Notwithstanding his great intelligence it was obvious that the Tsar found the instructions confusing. He was not helped by the anxiety of his wife and daughters writ large on their faces and betrayed by their nervous hands constantly clasping and unclasping. The Tsar tried to repeat the instructions but made several mistakes. 'It's no use, doctor,' he groaned in despair, 'I will never master it. Perhaps Mr Cambeuil can sit next to me and instruct me.'

'I am afraid not, sir. He has never driven a car before — in fact that was the first time he had been in a car.'

'Then all is lost, doctor. We must change clothes again and have faith in Premier Kerensky.'

'No, sir,' replied the doctor firmly. 'Only words directly from yourself can sting the British Government into action.'

'What you say may be true,' said the Empress, 'but it does not turn the Tsar into a chauffeur.'

Dr Watson pondered for a moment, his mind racing. 'There is a way, sir. I will come with you and show you what to do but it is very simple. Put the gears into neutral and put the advance-retard full on. It is marked on the steering wheel. The engine will start as it is still warm from my journey. Then put it into third gear — do not forget the clutch, and push the accelerator down, but be careful, the car will pick up speed quickly and may backfire.'

The Tsar repeated the instructions, twice. He was right both times. There was now hope. Gibbs and Cambeuil returned.

'Is all ready?' asked Gibbs, a smile masking his apprehension.

'I hope so,' replied the doctor earnestly.

The three Britons went to the door as the Royal Family took their leave of each other. The Britons simply shook hands.

As the doors opened, Watson became the Tsar and was immediately surrounded by soldiers. They would not allow him to go to the car, but he was allowed to descend halfway down the steps. 'We don't want you escaping us, Citizen Romanoff,' they jibed.

Colonel Kobylinsky stood by and observed the Tsar and the way he walked. Something was amiss.

Cambeuil and Gibbs descended the palace steps, the chauffeur a respectful two paces behind but he moved swiftly ahead and opened the door for his passengers. He then made as though to go to the driver's side but remembered to enter from the passenger door. For a long moment he looked at the controls of the great car. He moved the knobs and levers on the steering wheel but as he did so Watson could see that he had not put the gear lever on to neutral. If he put the advance-retard lever on to full without putting the gears into neutral the car would stall and their deception would be discovered. The advance-retard reached full and the engine burst into life, but it did not stall. The chauffeur had obviously put his foot on the clutch pedal at the last moment. He then reached for the gear lever but released the hand brake instead. If he took his foot from the clutch pedal now the car would start in a very low first gear and probably stall if he tried to negotiate the other gears. The car drew slowly away. It was travelling at less than five miles an hour, each individual cylinder's firing clearly discernible. The chauffeur revved slightly, the car's engine note increased but the speed remained low. As though in slow motion the car turned onto the drive, the spokes of each wheel barely blurred by speed.

Inquisitive soldiers left their posts and went to peer at the car and its driver, clad in such strange clothes. Watson's heart beat faster. Some Cossacks on their high-spirited horses rode round the car, whistling and shouting to each other. They were now halfway along the drive. Watson took a deep breath as the sluggish scene receded in perspective.

Three quarters of the drive, the car was now only a speck in the distance to Watson's straining eyes. Only a matter of yards to go to the gate.

Then there was a flash of red and a moment later the sound of a loud bang. The soldiers cocked their guns. The car had backfired! Had the Tsar tried to change gear? Another backfire! Watson's heart was in his mouth. A horse reared, the car swerved off the drive into soft soil. The engine revved, the wheels spun, the rear of the car fishtailed and skidded, catching the gate pillar a glancing blow. Watson broke into a cold sweat, the soldiers took aim. The next second took an hour as the car spun 180° in a grotesque adagio pirouette and faced back to the palace, its Parthenon grille glinting in the distance.

It was then that Watson felt the game was up. He had not shown the Tsar where reverse was and the gateway was too narrow for the car to turn fully.

Time stood still but the car did not. The grille grew slowly larger — it was coming back to the palace! Was the Tsar giving himself up? At a speed no more than walking pace the car returned to the palace steps. The chauffeur alighted and nimbly ascended the steps and in Oxford English announced to the surrogate Tsar, 'My sincerest apologies, Your Majesty, please send the British Embassy a full claim for the damages.'

Tsar and chauffeur bowed and Soviet soldiers raised their rifles above their heads — and cheered. The chauffeur swiftly descended the steps and leapt into the car. Driving slower than ever he finally steered the Ghost into the mists beyond Tsarkoe Selo.

'Thank God he did not use the foot brake,' thought Watson as he turned to rejoin the Royal Family who stood colourless on the top step. Surgeon Cambeuil calculated how he could dine out on the story for the rest of his life.

The next few days were full of difficulty for the new Tsar. Although he was cognizant of the old routine of the royal apartments the new conditions were alien to him, but the Tsarista was constantly at his shoulder to assist him. She advised him not to go for walks in the park on his own as the real Tsar had done. But the old soldier refused in case it was thought that the Tsar was afraid of his own people. He continued to cut firewood, stacking it in neat piles, watering the newly planted vegetables, and digging over the soil, all projects started by Nicholas himself.

In the evenings the family gathered to read to each other. Dr Watson's Russian improved as did the Romanoffs' understanding of the science of deduction.

Each day they waited for news, each day they were disappointed. Then one evening a group of soldiers burst into the room as the family was busily occupied sewing, knitting and reading. A sentry had seen someone signalling with two lights from the room. The soldiers looked threateningly at each member of the family. One of them approached the Grand Duchess Anastasia to see what she had been sewing. There was a cry from a sentry in the courtyard. The explanation of the mystery was that the lamp next to Grand Duchess Anastasia had two shades, one green and one red, so that each time she moved she obscured one of the lights. Grudgingly the guards departed.

'Why does he not come?' intoned the Tsaritsa. 'It is three weeks since we sent word to him.'

'Perhaps he did not believe us,' the doctor replied.

Before the sentence had fully left his lips the door burst open again and in strode the Russian Premier, a surprisingly spare man who seemed constantly on edge. He marched straight to the Tsar and looked hard at him. After several seconds of close scrutiny he smiled. 'So it is true, Dr Watson. You are now the Tsar. What are your terms?'

'Freedom for the Imperial family,' he replied.

'I too wish for that and have worked for it, but I cannot guarantee my own freedom!' he cried with emotion. 'The Bolsheviks aim to destroy us all. They are fanatics.'

'I can arrange for finance,' the doctor advised. 'With money from my Government, you will be able to pay the army to support you and destroy your Bolshevik enemies.'

'It is possible, but where is the Tsar?'

'On British soil.'

'Your Embassy?'

'That is correct.'

'This is very dangerous.'

'Indeed. If anything were to happen to him, while he was there, the British Empire would be forced to act.'

'And if anything happens to you the same result would follow?'

'I believe so.'

'This is blackmail.'

'No, merely concentrating the mind. The Provisional Government has vacillated too long.'

'I have spoken to Mr Gibbs and Sir George and agree with your idea. Pack in secret and take warm clothes with you. I will prepare everything.'

With that he turned on his heel and was gone.

'Can we trust him, Your Highness?' the doctor asked.

'My husband believes so,' she replied.

'Then so must we.'

'I don't like it,' reflected Sir George as he sat before the British Embassy fire. 'I don't like it at all. There are too many strident dissident voices in the Duma. There is even a Soviet now, dominated by Bolsheviks. And who is this Sverdlov who calls for the execution of the Tsar?'

The Tsar shrugged his shoulders. 'I do not know him, but it seems that there are many shadow people who form opinion here. We must move quickly.'

Meanwhile, Kerensky's preparations were almost complete as were Sverdlov's. Kerensky's plan was to take the Royal Family to Tobolsk, a complete backwater in NW Siberia where they would be safe from revolutionary fervour; Sverdlov envisaged a more permanent solution.

Jacob Sverdlov was an implacable enemy of the Romanoffs and there was no love lost between him and Kerensky. Like many Bolsheviks, Sverdlov was of Jewish stock, and he possessed a brain of astute political awareness and a ruthless intellect. He was President of the Central Executive Committee of the All Russian Congress of Soviets. It was also said that he could carry the whole of Congress's business in his head. (A worthy adversary for Mycroft Holmes.) He had developed a system of spies throughout the garrison and servants at Tsarkoe Selo, and he was willing to use them against fellow revolutionaries of any party as much as he was against the Tsar.

Kerensky kept the evacuation plans as secret as he could, but when he recruited soldiers for a new regiment to guard the Royal Family and gave them their uniforms as well as higher pay the soldiers themselves became worried. They feared that they were returning to the Front. The whisper was heard by Sverdlov who planned accordingly.

On the night of August 12th 1917 Kerensky arrived at Tsarkoe Selo to escort the Royal Family onto the train but Sverdlov's henchmen were at work. First the soldiers refused to help move the royal baggage until they were paid and the railwaymen refused to prepare a train. This gave Sverdlov's agents time to carry out their long rehearsed plans.

What did Sverdlov hope to gain from this?

Once in Sverdlov's power the Romanoffs would be imprisoned where no-one could reach them. It meant that they could become puppets but historical precedent suggested a more final fate. Cromwell had had Charles Stuart executed to remove the focus of opposition to this revolution, to unite his own forces so that they knew that there was no turning back, and to show all observers that he meant to carry his revolution to its logical conclusion by employing the most ruthless methods. His illegal, ungenerous, ignoble act had one virtue — success. It was a precedent that Sverdlov found compellingly attractive.

Kerensky and Kobylinsky urged and cajoled. The soldiers were paid to move the baggage. The railway workers set up the train but refused to drive it. Kerensky reported to the Tsar and after a brief consultation telephoned Petrograd. An hour later a heavy-shouldered man with long arms and brindled beard appeared at the marshalling yard and built up a head of steam in the locomotive that was to pull the carriages of the royal suite which bore Japanese flags and the legend 'Japanese Red Cross Mission'. Before long a procession of cars appeared surrounded by mounted Cossacks. The royal suite alighted and embarked on the train. One old retainer asked Kerensky in a loud voice that many overheard, 'How long are we to be in Tobolsk?'

The agitated and by now utterly exhausted Kerensky replied, 'Until the Assembly meets in November and then you shall all be free to go wherever you wish.'

Thus assured, the royal suite left on its journey to Tobolsk in the Siberian wastes. As the party left, Kerensky gave Kobylinsky a piece of paper. That piece of paper and the train driver were to save the lives of the entire royal suite.

The journey to Tobolsk takes four days and involves passage through many small villages. There is only one large town on the route, Perm, a day out from Petrograd.

On the train the daily routine returned to what it had been for the Royal Family before the Revolution, with tea at four a high spot of the day.

It was then that the children voiced their fears but Watson's stories from medical life of grave illnesses stoically borne and overcome acted as heartening cordials to depressed spirits. But they all missed the Tsar, their father.

When the train passed through villages the curtains were drawn at each window and no-one was allowed to show themselves.

At Perm the local officials insisted that the train stop. Honest farmers, these men did not like this secrecy. Their leader was a dignified old man with a white beard. He approached Kobylinsky who showed him the paper that Kerensky had given him. It read, 'Colonel Kobylinsky's orders are to be obeyed as if they were my own. Alexander Kerensky.' The old man rubbed his chin. 'I must consult with my council,' he replied.

'Why?' thundered the Colonel.

'We have received other orders,' came the reply.

'From whom?' continued the Colonel no less belligerently.

'Moscow.'

'Moscow?'

Before he could finish Arthur Rowbotham appeared. 'There's summat up here. I know these tracks. The points have been changed. If we go on now we go to Yekaterinberg, not Tobolsk.'

'Yekaterinberg,' gasped the Tsaritsa. 'But they hate us there. That is why we are being sent to Tobolsk.'

'Old man,' said Kobylinsky, his tone hardening. 'Show me your authority.'

The venerable figure took a piece of paper from his pocket and held it up.

'There is no official identification, old man,' snarled the Colonel. 'It hardly compares with a handwritten authority from the Premier of Russia. Alter those points immediately or it will be the worse for you.'

'I'll go and see that they do,' added Rowbotham. 'I won't be long.'

When they had gone, Colonel Kobylinsky turned to the Tsar and said, 'Thus it is that the honest are made dupes by evil men.' Watson's Russian was not quite up to that so he simply nodded sagely. 'The Jezail bullet still pains you, Dr Watson?' Kobylinsky asked in English.

'Only occasionally,' the doctor replied and regretted it instantly.

'I thought as much,' cried the Colonel triumphantly.

'You know me?' Watson asked.

'I have seen you in Petrograd. You are very good at billiards, I noticed in the Officers' Club.'

'What will you do with us now?' inquired the Tsaritsa apprehensively.

'My duty is to protect the Royal Family. I always do my duty.' He clicked his heels and saluted. Just at that moment there was a cry from outside.

'It's Rowbotham,' said Watson. 'He's in trouble.'

The two men rushed outside and saw Rowbotham being set upon by a group of men with scarves drawn up round their faces. The Lancastrian was putting up a good show as two men fell to his fists; the others fled when they saw help arriving.

'I think we'd best be going, gents,' the train driver cried, gasping for breath. 'They play it rough round 'ere.'

'What happened, man?' Watson urged.

'When I came out there were two fellows in the cab and another changing the points to Yekaterinberg. Yuri my relief driver is dead, and I feel a bit poorly.' With that he pitched forward, a knife jutting from his back.

They took him into the royal carriage and laid him on a soft bed. The Tsaritsa said that she and her daughters would nurse him as they had nursed many a wounded soldier at the Front and indeed were fully qualified nurses. The Colonel was in a towering rage which none of the locals dared to exacerbate. A relief crew of drivers was soon assembled and the train made off for Tobolsk.

Watson's admiration for the Royal Family grew as they showed genuine concern for their charge. He came to revel in their company and Alexis became like the son he never had. Alexis grew fitter and stronger despite the tedium of travel and Nagorny became the doctor's friend although they had few words of each other's language.

When the suite arrived in Tobolsk they were reasonably well housed in the old governor's residence. Security was not too strict and conditions were bearable.

Then in November the dam burst. Kerensky fell from power as the Bolsheviks took over. November, the month they had hoped would see their freedom, instead became the bitterest time of all as it was snatched away and hope floundered.

In Petrograd, the day that Kerensky had resigned all power, Sir George Buchanan went for a walk to the Winter Palace. He noticed that life appeared normal. Shops, markets, restaurants, even cinemas, were all open as though nothing had happened, but Tsar Nicholas in the British Embassy had a different view.

'I have condemned Dr Watson to death. I must return to my family.'

Despite Sir George's remonstrations he would not budge. He felt that the British Government had no sympathy for him and that they would not lift a finger to help him. He also knew that the Bolsheviks hated him.

'If you do not help me to return to my family, Sir George, I will go to the Supreme Soviet and declare myself before them.' In the face of such obduracy Sir George could only acquiesce.

News had just reached the Embassy that Arthur Rowbotham had died of his injuries and so Sir George arranged for a train to go to Tobolsk to bring back the remains of the valiant engineer. Bolsheviks stood aside at the sight of the Union flag and the train made fast time. The Tsar hoped that he had not changed too much.

The coffin for the driver's remains was very large and

heavy. So much so that the newer more militant Bolshevik guards insisted on checking it for a false compartment. In their keenness to disturb the dead they missed the quick. With Kobylinsky's help the second substitution was easier than the first. Only the faithful Colonel recognized that the 'Tsar' had recovered from his limp, although he also noted that the Dr Watson who had alighted from the train had had a limp as well as the one who embarked on it. The Tsar was a very talented man, for everything except being a Tsar. He was Russia's Charles Stuart.

The train did not return to Petrograd; instead it made for Murmansk where the HMS *Torquay* and a Scottish naval surgeon awaited the cortège.

As soon as he boarded the train Dr Watson shaved off his beard leaving only his small moustache. Nicholas had brought Watson's bag. This the doctor unstitched and secreted into the lining an envelope bearing the crest of the Romanoff given to him by Grand Duchess Marie as he left.

The journey was a lugubrious one. The flat landscape which was lashed into featureless uniformity by the icy winds from the Arctic reflected his spirits. Despite the fact that he was going home he could not help thinking of the family he had become a part of and which he was leaving behind to the mercies of bigoted, ignorant self-seekers who operated under the banner of revolution. When his thoughts left them for a moment he had no light relief to comfort him. In the next compartment lay the corpse of Arthur Rowbotham accompanied by his sobbing wife and children. Russia was a mournful place.

The monotonous motion of the train across the plains sent Watson to sleep when at last he could dream of Mary, Baker Street, Holmes and happier times, but perhaps because of his army training and adventures with Sherlock Holmes he sensed danger. The dozing Holmes of whom he dreamt jumped to his feet and shook Watson's shoulder. 'Look out, old chap. Look out,' his vision pleaded vehemently.

Watson awoke to a rough shaking of his shoulder. He looked up and saw three rifles pointing at his chest. 'Papers, papers,' shouted his assailant.

'In my case,' replied a nettled doctor. The leader of the men turned to the case and rummaged through it. 'You are Dr Watson?' he asked suavely.

'I am who my papers say I am.'

'Dr John Ross?'

'That's right. Dr John Ross.'

'You know this Dr Watson?'

'I have knowledge of his reputation.'

'If you tell us where he is you will earn a great reward and the friendship of Soviet Russia,' the interrogator urged.

'I'm sorry, but I cannot help you.'

At that moment there was a scream from the next compartment. It was Mrs Rowbotham. The searchers had opened her husband's coffin; they obviously wanted their man very badly. Watson looked out of the window; it was a desolate spot.

'Now look here,' he cried. 'We are all British citizens and we are expected in Murmansk by the Royal Navy. If we are not there by this evening there will be serious consequences.'

The leader of the group tugged his goatee beard as though debating with himself his course of action. At last he waved his hand, 'You may go. Tell your people how we have hurt no-one and want only justice for all, Dr Ross.'

'I will convey your message,' came the stiff reply.

Later that evening the dim glow of Murmansk and the lights of HMS *Torquay* were a more wonderful sight than any Northern light. As he negotiated the gangplank Dr

Watson smiled broadly. At that same moment Jacob Sverdlov was grinding his teeth in Moscow's ancient Kremlin and Mycroft Holmes sat purring contentedly in his armchair at the Diogenes.

Envoi.

What happened to Watson's scheme to take the Royal Family across Russia, one which Kerensky had obviously thought sound considering the way he had checked out their train on its journey to Tobolsk? Mr Sidney Gibbs succeeded in achieving it some time later.

What happened to the Royal Family? That is another story in which a tall, dark haired, well educated man with long thin hands named Vasily Vaslevich Yakovlev takes a prominent place.

Finally, what were the two letters that Stamford found in the lining of Watson's bag?

One asked forgiveness and offered him a Knighthood. He accepted one and not the other.

The other contained a photograph of the Tsar (or was it Watson?) at Tsarkoe Selo sitting on a tree stump being guarded by three soldiers standing to attention. On the back was written 'Vice versa. N.' with beneath that a row of matchstick men, viz.

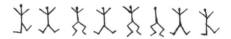

accompanied by A & A, and finally: прощание — OTMA.

Whatever else might have happened, Dr John H. Watson and the Romanoffs never met again.

Part Three

A Scholar's Appendix

The Solitary Student

'The proper study of mankind is man,' Watson had said to me, quoting Alexander Pope, after we had left Sherlock Holmes working among his chemicals in the laboratory at Bart's and walked together towards Watson's hotel on the afternoon of their introduction to each other. It was obvious that Watson had found Holmes a very interesting person particularly his 'little peculiarity' of being able to 'find things out'. I could see that this 'piquant mystery' had given Watson something to get his teeth into after the vacuous nature of his previous existence in London on his army pension. As it happens I already knew the answer to the mystery. My comment at the time, 'A good many people have wanted to know how he finds things out,' should not be taken to mean that I was in ignorance of Holmes's new science of deduction, but I could see how Watson had bucked-up now that he felt himself to be involved in something singular and I did not wish to dampen his spirits by giving away the answer before he had a chance to solve the riddle for himself. It was just what he needed to help him recover from the dreadful recent past in Afghanistan and no doctor could have prescribed a better tonic for him. Thus I left Watson unenlightened as to Holmes's secret not out of my own ignorance or malice, but out of kindness.

As you probably know I am not mentioned as appearing again in *The Study of Scarlet* after effecting the initial introduction, and so it was. I had been involved in some foolish horseplay which had had some unpremeditated yet nonetheless awful repercussions and was soon to leave the country. I did not get a medical degree then — that came later at a far larger university even than that of London, although beginning with the same letter. I was waiting for a berth on a ship to take me to Australia to rebuild my life and serve as a penance for those whose lives I had inadvertently blighted. Ironically I was in fact acting on Sherlock Holmes's advice, which was to be the same advice that he subsequently gave to big Bob Ferguson (the ex-Richmond three-quarter who had thrown Watson over the ropes at Old Deer Park) concerning his son Jack at the conclusion of the case of *The Sussex Vampire*. Three days later I was on my way to the Antipodes and a series of adventures that were to pull me up by my bootstraps — but I digress. There is time for me to outline those events later, it is Holmes and Watson who properly fill the centre stage.

Holmes had taken rooms in London during his first two years at university, not after as some seem to believe. He clearly stated later in *The Gloria Scott* that after he left the Trevors at Donnithorpe in Norfolk he went up to his London rooms where he spent seven weeks working out a few experiments in organic chemistry. This was his first long vacation, he having made Victor Trevor's acquaintance during the Lent term of his first year at College, not his second. (Just because Holmes said that Trevor was the only friend he made in his two years at college, it does not follow that he made him in his second year — as we shall see.) After the *Gloria Scott* case, Trevor left university and became a Terai tea planter where Matilda Briggs and I were to meet him later.

Holmes's second year at university — yes, it was Oxford by the way — was spent in even deeper thought and greater solitude than his first. It was during that academic session after prolonged personal agonizing that Holmes decided to act on old Trevor Senior's words and become a detective; but not just any sort of detective. He would become the world's first ever consulting detective.

However, I am going too fast.

What light can I throw on Holmes's origins? His date of birth I never did discover* — it may well be Twelfth Night. Watson did leave clues for us just as Holmes did for Watson when first they met. As to his origins, he was from East Anglia. On this both Holmes and Watson have left us clues in the narratives. When Victor Trevor's bull terrier froze on Holmes's ankle one morning whilst he was on the way down to chapel, the wound was so bad that he was laid up for ten days as a result. Victor Trevor came to see him each day to inquire as to his health and they became friends. Holmes said that in many ways they were opposites. On the one hand Holmes was fond of moping in his own rooms working out his own methods of thought, and on the other Trevor was a hearty, full-blooded fellow, full of spirit and energy. Yet they had one thing in common which Holmes names — 'he was as friendless as I' — and 'some subjects in common' that he does not name. The main subjects that they had in common were their East Anglian origins and background which included the hunting, shooting and fishing that could be enjoyed on the Broads and Fens, and an unfortunate home life with regard to their mothers

*I suggest St Crispin's Day, 25th October, because of his love of Henry V's 'the game's afoot'.

which was to make them both wary of women, but never unchivalrous as some have suggested, for the rest of their lives.

As a lot of my information concerning Holmes came to me from Victor Trevor perhaps it would be more appropriate to put it in his own words as far as a nonogenarian can remember a conversation that took place some seventy years ago on the verandah of a tea planter's house in the Terai between two young expatriates who conversed about mutual friends in the Old Country while sipping a sundowner as the ship of one was being loaded with the tea of the other. Nonetheless I shall try and if the words are not verbatim, there are no conscious errors in the text, unless that is Trevor passed any errors on to me, intentionally or otherwise.

Victor Trevor's Narrative

'My father was a newcomer to Norfolk. He had made his fortune in the goldfields of Australia and had come back to England to enjoy his hard-earned wealth. East Anglia, and Norfolk in particular, were regarded as somewhat of a backwater and Donnithorpe even more so, being a small hamlet of less than a dozen houses just north of Langmere in the country of the Broads. It was as though he were trying to hide himself away for some reason. He married into the large Norfolk Matthews family, his wife coming from a rather poor branch of that family, but after a whirl-wind courtship they were married and had set up their home in the best house in Donnithorpe. After several years my old governor must have thought Fortune had smiled on him. He had a wife, two children, a fine house, was respected locally for his good deeds and charitable works and was a Justice on the local bench where he became celebrated for his leniency in an age of legal barbarity.

'As I grew up my father and I became very close. He would often take me out on the Broads hunting wild fowl, or fishing. We would sometimes spend whole days and nights away from home. It was a great adventure for me which he would enhance by telling me exciting stories of his days in the goldfields of Ballarat.

'My mother's relatives would often come and visit us and would take full advantage of my father's generous hospitality while patting me on the head and saying what a fine boy I was growing into, "quite the little country squire." They would often ask my father about his origins but he would shrug off their rustic inquisitiveness with a comment like "it's nowhere near as interesting as the history of your long line," or, if they became more inquisitorial he would simply say, "why, London, of course, like I've said before."

'My mother was typical of her class, not very well educated — our fine library was like another world to her — and more concerned with social advancement than the acquisition of knowledge. Of course, it was, as I see now, a marriage of convenience. My mother's name and connections gave my father an instant mantle of respectability and his money was a welcome fillip to the Matthews "cadet" line.

'It was only slowly that I became aware of the tension between them. I noticed it more when I was at boarding school. Each holiday at home would have a more charged atmosphere than the last, despite the outward appearances and the fuss that was made of me. Finally it dawned on me. It was a marriage without love. Many of my schoolfriends came from similar loveless matches, but it was a shock to realize that the same applied to myself. It could have survived better I suppose if my mother had not been so bored. She had very little with which to occupy her time, until the birth of my sister some years later, and so took to criticizing my father about everything from his table manners to his shoes. She found a thousand small faults in him. At first I am sure it was more out of capricious boredom than malice, but my obvious love of my father and our little expeditions made her more vicious. She felt left out.

'My father organized shopping trips to Langmere for her, weekends when there was open house and she could play the part of hostess. Even the birth of a daughter whom she could cosset seemed to only partly assuage her ill humour.

'Unfortunately that turned to ashes in all our mouths when, on a visit to Birmingham — a special treat for my mother, my little sister contracted diphtheria and died. She was only three years old.

'My mother's instant reaction in her grief was that my father was blaming her for my sister's death — it had been a trip to please her after all. My father assured her that nothing was further from his mind and was kindness itself to her.

'Perhaps as I look back that had been part of the trouble. My father had indulged my mother's whims too much and she had become spoilt. Perhaps also she had been unhappy from the start of their marriage, feeling as though she had been bought, so that her self-respect was cheapened, and having so much leisure, her somewhat limited mind created all sorts of fantasies about people talking behind her back. Her people did the rather novel thing of emigrating to Ireland where they, in fact, prospered, but it had the effect of leaving her more isolated. Thus she sought to assert her independence by trying my father's patience to the limit. She was more the child than I. I tended to support my father by joining him on our hunting excursions. This of course contributed to the downward spiral of ill feeling.

'It was on one of these trips that two things happened, the one insignificant to a young boy of fourteen, the other profound.

'As we paddled our flat-bottom boat in search of wild fowl we heard the sharp report of a gun to the north of us and the splashing and barking of a retriever as he went about his master's business. Eventually in the distance my father could make out a tall figure. He asked Neb, one of the stable boys who acted as general guide and helpmate on some of these trips, who it was. "Oh, that be Mr Sherrinford of Holme Hale. He's a rum 'un." Exactly what that meant we never found out as a loud hailer was heard calling our names. "No more shooting for Mr Sherrinford," said Neb as we watched the wild fowl disappear at the unaccustomed noise.

'It turned out it was Neb's father who had come after us with bad news. There had been an accident and my mother was dying. How a country woman could have been so clumsy in getting the bucket out of a well, no-one could understand. However, the fact remained that she had fallen down it and had cracked her skull and caved her ribs in. We reached her only just in time.

'It is here that my narrative becomes most painful. Despite all the wrongs and hurts, mostly unintentional I was sure, though nonetheless spiteful, she was still my mother, but we parted with harsh words and remained unreconciled. Her imminent death had made her reproachful and proud, and it scarred me for life.

'After that my father and I were even closer to each other and there was a tear in his eye when I chose to go to Oxford and not the nearer Cambridge. However, he gave me a bull terrier and said it was to be my mascot which would bring me luck.

'Luck? Whatever else it brought me, it brought me Sherlock Holmes.

'My first visit to Holmes's rooms after my dog had latched onto his ankle was only a very brief formal affair. He looked so pale and thin that I thought it best not to tax him too much. However, I went the next day and he was still pale and thin but much more talkative so I stayed longer. The visits got longer as we warmed to each other as we spoke about tutors, boxing, dogs, food and wine. It was very much to my surprise that one day he greeted me by saying, "Of course, how foolish of me, Trevor of Donnithorpe. You must know Sherrinford."

' "Sherrinford?" I replied, puzzled. "I am sure that I have never heard of the place."

' "It is not a place, it is a person. My uncle Sherrinford Holmes of Holme Hope, near Swaffham, in Norfolk."

'It was only after some memory searching that I could recall any such reference in my experiences. Then I was back in the boat with my father and Neb on the awful day when my mother had died. I felt a chill go through me; "see a Holmes and lose a parent," I foolishly thought, unaware of my prophecy.

'After that we were soon happily chatting about Norfolk although in fact our homes were the entire Broads apart and both very isolated, but we spoke like old neighbours about fowl brought down and fish that had escaped. I asked why we had never met before. Apart from the obvious reason of distance there was another reason. Holmes told me that when his brother Mycroft went to university his parents had taken him away. He was just eleven at the time. Perhaps it was the way he said it but I felt that there was more to it than he was revealing but I let it pass. As we talked I then realized that he seemed to be telling me more about myself than I had let slip. He simply chuckled at my dismay.

'On one occasion Reginald Musgrave drifted into Holmes's room to borrow a book and they chatted together amiably enough if a little formally. I did not like Musgrave very much myself — too proud by half, I always thought — yet Holmes would always defend him. He said that what I took for pride was merely an attempt to cover an extreme natural diffidence. If that was so I never really saw it, but then Holmes was like that. He could defend someone and be tactful to that person's critic all in one. Despite his love for solitude he could be charm and tact itself when he needed to be. More than once I thought of him as a chemical compound made up of Anglo-Saxon reserve and tenacity with a dash of Gallic charm and unpredictability. He could have been successful with the ladies but his mind was on other things.

'One day when others had noticed how we had struck up a friendship, I was asked, "Do you know how he does it?"

'"Does what?" I asked.

'"Knows so much about everyone? He frightened the life out of Dodgson the Mathematician the other day by saying that he would get better results for his efforts if he used a wider aperture with longer exposure and less silver nitrate when he was developing his plates. He thought no-one knew he had a camera."

'I had to admit to being as mystified as the others.

'When he first visited my rooms for tiffin I asked him if he could tell me something more about myself. He seemed to take the room in at a glance and said that I came from a house which had little residual female influence in it, suggesting a widower at the head of it. He also pointed out that there had been a sister but her existence had been equally without duration or influence. I was amazed at his revelations because despite our increasing friendship I had not mentioned my little sister to him, but I was too offended by his cold manner to ask him to explain his conclusions. He obviously saw that I was deeply hurt and immediately apologized to me in the warmest terms which came as a complete contradiction to his earlier machine-like inhuman manner. Our deep friendship started from that moment. We never discussed our families' histories again.

'Holmes was a very serious student who worked very hard at his subject. Like many younger brothers he was destined for the church. However, charming as he could be, I could not imagine him officiating at christenings, tea parties and fund-raising sales for good causes. His study was somehow too fierce for such a placid round. He wanted to learn the Truth. This involved the study of the original Bible languages (Holmes was a very remarkable linguist), calligraphy, manuscripts, other contemporary sources, as well as the close study of ethics, logic and philology. His researches led him to believe that Mark's Gospel was the earliest of the four and that the ending to it was written by another, later hand. If this were true it would bring the story of the Resurrection into question and with it the whole foundation of Christianity and those societies which based themselves on it. He could find no real satisfaction in the solutions of his Dons. The Church told him that this discovery required an even greater act of faith on his part. This was a trying time indeed for him. He had contemplated becoming a missionary but how could he if his faith was so eroded by doubt?

'He left Oxford for the Easter vacation weighed down by doubt. I learned later that he had stayed with his brother Mycroft in Montague Street and had spent a great deal of his time in the Reading Room of the British Museum having been furnished with suitable letters of recommendation by his college to enable the under-aged reader to gain admittance.

'When he returned for the third term he looked to have cleared some doubt from his mind but there was still something nagging at him. I tried to bring him out of himself. I asked about his brother Mycroft: he was apparently as slothful as ever and wished to get some rooms near Pall Mall as he had had an idea about a club he was thinking of forming with people he was glad to never have to speak to and did not wish to be too far away from it. This man sounded incredible! "Oh, he is," remarked Sherlock, answering my expression, not any vocal exclamation. "He is quite the most brilliant man in London."

'At the mention of Mycroft, his brother seemed to brighten up considerably. We decided to spar for a few rounds. I was considered a large strong fellow but I could never master Holmes's straight classical left jab nor his rapier-like right. I was amazed at the strength of one so slight, but not at all surprised to discover that he was a very good swordsman. His blade was an extension of his arm.

'Over the weeks Holmes seemed to relax more after the tension of the Lent term which had started with a bull terrier gripping his ankle and ended with a remarkable piece of Biblical exegesis. We often went on walks around town and on one occasion he asked me to take him round Oxford in a cab which was shuttered and in which he was blindfold to see if I could catch him out on any of the street names. He was 100% correct.

'On another occasion we visited a fair in St Giles, only a small affair, not the proper one, probably just a last vestige of the "mops" they used to have. Here he dazzled the fortune teller by telling her all about herself and where she would end up if she did not change some of her ways. She fell back in amazement at his revelations and all she could say (although it was more of a shriek) was, " 'Ere, I fought I was the fortune teller round 'ere."

'Some of the more speculative students thought that Holmes had some sort of supernatural powers and they compared him in his physique, talents and violin virtuosity with another similar man of whom the same slanders were spoken — Nicolo Paganini. Holmes's reply to that was always a chuckle and an enigmatic smile which provoked even more idle curiosity.

'It was that summer that Holmes came to stay for a month with us at Donnithorpe. I will never be able to forget it. That first incredible series of deductions about my father as we sat over a glass of port after dinner. He started by saying that there was not very much that he could deduce except that during the last twelve months my father had gone in fear of attack, that he had boxed in his youth a great deal, had done a lot of digging, that he had visited New Zealand and Japan, and that he had been intimately associated with someone whose initials were JA and whom he afterwards was eager entirely to forget.

'This resulted in my old governor pitching forward among the nutshells in a dead faint. From that day on he eyed Holmes with suspicion which cast a bit of a damper on things. Later when a man calling himself Hudson appeared things got worse. My father gave him an excellent job with hardly any responsibilities and was repaid by this man behaving in a terrible way, getting drunk and behaving badly with the other staff — particularly the women. I was all for throwing him out on his ear but my dear father would have nothing of it. One day he insulted my father and I threw the wretch out of the room. Then to my utter amazement my father asked if I would apologize to Hudson! I refused point blank.

'When this Hudson finally slunk away still I had not apologized and he looked very threateningly at my father, saying he was going to see Mr Beddoes in Hampshire. My father remained in a high state of agitation and finally received an incomprehensible note about "game", "fly-paper" and your "hen-pheasant's life"! My father took one look at it and had a stroke. I wired Holmes immediately; only he could unravel this mystery — and he was also my only friend in the world. He came immediately and soon cracked the code of the message — "The game is up. Hudson has told all. Fly for your life."

'My father had left a document for me which he had written when that devil Hudson was in our house. It revealed that my father was not named Trevor but he was a James Armitage who had been transported to Australia for using money that was not his own to repay "a debt of honour". He expected to be able to replace the money with no-one the wiser, but there was a premature examination of the books before he could make good the loss and the penalty was transportation in the *Gloria Scott*.

'Worse was to follow. There was a mutiny by the prisoners and after a night of carnage they had taken control of the ship. Those, including my father, who had had enough of the killing were set adrift in an open boat. Later there was an explosion and the *Gloria Scott* sank with only one survivor, Hudson, a young seaman. After my father and a friend named Evans (later to be Beddoes) had made their escapes and their fortunes, they returned to England where this Hudson blackmailed them.

'You can imagine how I felt, Surgeon Stewart.* Then perhaps you cannot (I certainly could, Mr Victor Trevor, believe me). No matter — Donnithorpe was now a cruel jest to me. My whole family dead, despite their good intentions, and I was not even really Victor Trevor but

---

*I was travelling under an assumed name at the time for reasons which will become clear later.

Victor Armitage. I had no family, no household and now no name. I was heartbroken by it all and could not face any more of Oxford or of England. Thus you find me here, planting tea in the Terai.

'Whichever way I look at my experiences I feel that my life has been blighted. I have wealth with this plantation but what will happen if I go back to England? How will I know whether I am wanted for my money or myself? My wealth will make me the prey of fortune hunters. I despair of happiness.'

Stamford Resumes

Just then a boy came up to the verandah to inform us that the ship was loaded and it was time for me to board. I could not leave young Trevor like this, therefore I told him two things which I hoped would sustain him. First, I told him Holmes's new address in Baker Street. Second, I told him that if his old governor had needed an epitaph he could ask for no finer one than to be remembered as the man who gave Sherlock Holmes the advice that he was missing his vocation if he did not become a detective. Holmes admitted that it was the first time that he had ever felt that a profession might be made out of what up to then had been the merest hobby. Trevor's words might have lost Biblical Studies a great scholar but they gained the world its greatest detective.

What happened to Holmes next? As I have already pointed out he spent quite some time agonizing over old Trevor's words. The Bible or the detection of crime?

He sought out Samuel Dodgson and enjoyed the cut and thrust of logical debate, the beauties and complexities of higher mathematics. Life at Oxford could be so pleasant and he was young — was there need of any decision just yet? Why not just drift with Isis and be borne on her foaming wings to easier victories?

He brooded over his family. His father was in Sussex, his mother in France, and his brother in Montague Street. Once again he felt alone. He made a list of all the things in favour of his continuing his Biblical Studies and all those things which could be regarded as against this course of action. He did the same for a career in criminal detection.

None could doubt his abilities in either field. Holmes had already formulated the idea that to the logician modesty is as great a departure from the truth as the exaggeration of one's powers, and so sought the answer to his problem in cold reasoning and logic. Later he was to say[*] that there is nothing in which deduction is so necessary as in religion — 'It can be built up as an exact science by the reasoner.' But where had his reasoning and deduction got him? It had led to doubt and he felt that to lead a life in which he caused others to doubt would make of faith a mockery. There was only one honourable course open to him — he must fight crime and by so doing bring succour, not confusion, into the lives of those less gifted than himself.

Now began a period of frantic activity. What was necessary to make him fulfil his natural gifts? What could he study in order to make him fully proficient? Again he made a list, this time of those subjects which would be useful and those which would be of no use. Those that he considered of the most use were chemistry, anatomy, botany (particularly poisons, and possibly dyes), geology (i.e. a practical knowledge of soils as they occur on the surface and immediate sub-surface throughout his chosen area; theories of

_____
[*] *The Naval Treaty.*

rock formations were not to be considered but their where-abouts known if he should require such knowledge), the crimes of the last hundred years in detail (those of any earlier period to be confined to his reference section). Law and politics also featured on the list, the former as a practical necessity, the latter as an unavoidable chore. (A crime is a crime and politics merely useful as a source of motives for crime not as a study in itself.) Against this he set those subjects which could only be studied at the risk of overburdening the brain's retrieval abilities — literature, philosophy and astronomy. Harsh on philosophy perhaps, including as it did in Holmes's mind religion, but a cruel necessity, as Cromwell said of an earlier truncation. What else could there be of use to him in his new career, he asked himself? Fitness of limb certainly. Then with a smile he picked up his violin and mused, 'all work and no play will indeed make Sherlock very dull.'

Thus armed he went to see his tutors to see if he could be placed on another degree programme. They scratched their heads, tutted, removed spectacles and rubbed rheumy old eyes, tugged at threadbare gowns, whistled through their teeth, shuffled in their seats, referred Holmes to each other, or simply threw up their hands. In other words they revealed the classic symptoms of academic impotence.

Once again Holmes was on his own. He resigned his place in college but it was not accepted. His work on Bible exegesis was too highly regarded for him to be allowed to escape that easily. The Dons had hoped that he would grow out of this new, strange notion and return to the Church which after all in the past had been God's canopy that had sheltered many a singular soul. Holmes shrugged his shoulders — a Gallic gesture inherited from the Vernets which he rarely resorted to again. He had no wish to be disrespectful to his teachers and so kept his own council.

The Christmas of '74 saw him back in Montague Street again. Mycroft was as sedentary as ever, the first signs of corpulence already tugging at his mighty waistcoat. They lunched at Mycroft's window (Mycroft had no wish to climb stairs to his brother's rooms) and watched life go by outside. They played the game that they had first played as boys. Then they had called it 'guessing the job', now it was 'the study of mankind'. Once again Sherlock could only marvel at his brother's superior observation and deduction. Doubt crept into his mind, perhaps the Dons were right after all. A voice broke into his thoughts: 'Bib Studs and the responsibility of Empire to convert the fuzzy-wuzzy not cracked up to what you expected it to be, Sherlock?'

Holmes turned and smiled thinly at his brother. 'Well, the reasoning was easy enough, my dear boy, it is your resolution of the problem that lies in the balance.' Mycroft smiled at his younger brother.

Holmes pondered again. 'You have just missed a recently retired ship's surgeon who has done service in the Arctic and who lives with his sister, Mycroft.'

'Sisters, Sherlock, surely.'

'You see, Mycroft, how can I become anything to do with crime detection when I am but a pale shadow of yourself?'

'My dear Sherlock, you do yourself a grave disservice. When our parents suggested that I became a journalist or a diplomat, I blanched. I was hoping for a career in mathematics, but you know how I antagonized my tutors with my little pranks. They would recommend me for nothing, except perhaps as an army tutor to coach failed entrants or as a very junior accounts clerk somewhere obscure. Fortunately I had the foresight to choose the latter career. Coaching mentally deficient officer material is far more tiring than auditing governmental accounts. Thus I make my way with my figures, and observe for a pastime. A hippopotamus comfortable in his warm river, immobile yet observing with his little eyes all that washes past him. You, on the other hand, my dear Sherlock, have energy. You always wanted to go off doing things when you were younger. I had hoped that you would grow out of it, but alas it was not to be. If you wish to be a missionary an empire awaits you. If you wish to fight crime, London is at your doorstep.'

What was Mycroft suggesting? Sherlock looked at his brother's beaming face and the Cheshire cat came immediately to mind. 'Did you know Dodgson, Mycroft? If you did you will be immortal.' Mycroft continued to beam.

'I think it may rain later, Sherlock, feel free to borrow one of my umbrellas but I suggest that you wear a hat instead so that you can keep your hands free.'

Sherlock nodded and in a few moments was proofed against the weather and gone.

London in 1874 was the centre of the world's largest empire. Not only that, it was the banking capital of world commerce and a leading cog in Britain's claim to be the workshop of the world. At the many settings of the sun throughout the entire globe, loyal servants of Victoria would toast the Old Country and wish that they were back there taking in a play or a musical show or dining in any of a dozen renowned restaurants or just walking along the Strand or dropping into their club in St James. London was the largest city in the world, a mighty beast of a city of over four million souls, more than the entire population of the Antipodes. Just then Holmes trod in a large dollop of horse dropping. He smiled ruefully as he stamped his foot clean. London was also a place in which it paid to keep one's eyes open.

From Montague Street Holmes headed south-west to Soho by way of the 'rabbit warren' Seven Dials, Shaftesbury Avenue and Piccadilly Circus. From there he headed towards the recently completed Embankment via the Haymarket, Trafalgar Square and Northumberland Avenue. Turning east he walked the length of the Embankment before leaving the River Thames and making for the Royal Exchange. He was approaching unknown land. He had heard stories of the mysterious Orient but London's East End was no less unexplored by him. Holmes resolved to see for himself and test out the truth of the stories that he had heard, suspecting them to be in error. He toured Aldgate, Whitechapel and, turning for home, Spitalfields. He returned to Montague Street via Bishopsgate, Threadneedle Street, Poultry Lane, diverting from Cheapside to explore Ironmonger Lane and Wood Street, thence past St Paul's, Newgate Street, the Holborns, turning into Leather Lane and Clerkenwell Road — finally finding himself back in Bloomsbury.

Holmes had been out for several hours and when he returned to his rooms in Montague Street it was quite dark. Mycroft looked as though he had not moved from his chair but a crumb of biscuit in a fold of his ever expanding waistcoat suggested that he had at least moved his mouth in order to eat. Mycroft's face was still beaming as Sherlock entered and sat opposite him.

'I perceive that you have also lost a button from your coat as well as some blood from your lip.'

'Your advice was well-founded, Mycroft, but I should have taken a cane with me.'

'It was as bad as that, Sherlock?'

'The actuality was worse than anything I had imagined from perusing the daily newspapers.'

'Yes, it is more difficult to retain sang froid in the face of the more elemental forces. And?'

'Then your powers are failing you, brother Mycroft?'

'It is missionary work, I take it?'

'Indeed it is, and London shall be my territory.'

Thus is was that Sherlock Holmes's mind was finally resolved. That one walk around the streets of the Empire's mighty metropolis during the season of goodwill was enough to convince him of his calling.

Later he was to tell me how it had reminded him of the accounts of Spain in the seventeenth century. Spain at that time was in possession of the largest empire that the world had ever known. Gold, silver, precious stones flooded into Seville from the New World. Yet every eye witness account remarked on the enormous disparity between the amount of wealth coming into Spain and the grinding poverty of its people. That was London in 1874.

That day the city had been shrouded in fog as it was so often; a mixture of smoke from a million coal fires, some of it of very poor quality, steam from factories which included soap, phosphorus matches, dyeworks and iron foundries, as well as the mist from the river and the odours from a million decomposing objects from human corpses to horse dung. When the wind and the rain for once forced that foul mix away, they brought with them not fresh air from the fields of the home counties but a different menace called 'London Mud', sticky soot which stuck to everything from windows to clothes to skin and which gave off a pungent odour when anywhere near a heat source.

London certainly seemed to lay claim to its own individual climate. It could also lay claim to being two cities, the west and the east being roughly divided at London Bridge. The west was prosperous and self-satisfied, the east was to remind me of Calcutta for its poverty and deprivation. Both were united, however, by being riddled with crime and moral decay.

During the December of 1874 alone the records were to show that ninety-six bodies were found floating in the river with their throats either cut or bearing the unmistakable evidence of strangulation. A favourite crime was the abduction of heiresses for ransom and sometimes even white slavery in a place far removed from that of their birth. Many believed in the existence of secret societies from as far afield as Naples, Shanghai, Kiev and Chicago. Strange, demented fiends with springed heels were said to wait for nightfall and then prey on their hapless victims.

London was a dangerous place to live for another reason. It was a centre of accidents. People were crushed by coaches, fell off high ladders or through rotten trap-doors, were boiled by molten metal, were caught up in coach wheels or horses' reins and dragged to their deaths, succumbed to the impure atmosphere of industry and congestion, or were first mutilated by unguarded machinery and then died in agony through loss of blood or infection.

In the poorer quarters there was often not the cheapest of whale-oil lamps to bring light to the darkness. What would have been revealed could only have horrified the onlooker. Peoples of all races and ages barefoot and in rags huddled together for warmth, for whom Christmas only meant a particularly cold and dark period of the year as they fought to survive. They had no star to guide them. For such as these crime was a way of life and a means to the end of survival. A code of honour grew up so that informing to authority as represented by the Metropolitan Police Force was regarded as the worst possible crime to this community within a community.

Not that the forces of law and order could be much respected in 1874. Three years later the so-called Trial of the Detectives revealed the corruption that existed at the heart of the police force. Forensic science was as unknown as the word itself was foreign-sounding. To be sure of a conviction the culprit had to be caught 'red-handed'.

Once the deed was done the odds favoured the criminal.

The richer areas might have been able to afford proper street lighting but crime flourished nonetheless. It was not so much 'survival' crime as 'leisured' crime. Gaming and vice were the two most common. There were over four thousand clubs and brothels in the City of London itself — an area then much smaller than it is now. Gaming was regarded as almost respectable but it ruined many a man and led to suicides, blackmail, ruin and even murder. Many a black sheep flocked to St James to take advantage of his fellow degenerates. The Haymarket dealt in a different produce. Despite the prohibitions on such a traffic, women and children could still be bought and sold almost openly. They would then become for a few short years the sexual playthings of a group of moneyed dissipates eager for new sensations before becoming the washed-up jetsam on the barren shingle of poverty. There were highly organized vice rings which supplied the needs of the wealthy and most girls from the poor districts willingly became a part of them in order 'to put a bit by for later' before their looks faded and their favours became less valued.

As we have seen, Holmes was not interested in politics *per se*. He was not moved by what he saw to be a social reformer. Future readers looking back on London in this time will be shocked by the sights that I have outlined — if not them then certainly the smells — and they might be shocked by Holmes's reaction to the former. Young, late-twentieth-century readers with a century of reform, liberalism and socialism behind them might wonder why their hero did not champion the cause of the poor with a missionary zeal. In a way, he did. He recognized that his talents fitted him to be a crime detector, although his definition of a crime was often at variance with the legal definition of the period, and so in good Victorian tradition he sought to use his talents to the maximum. He was a man of his time in that respect. If he appears slightly cold to us now, then that was how he was. The years should not obscure Sherlock Holmes's sincere motives to combat crime whether committed by a duke or a destitute. He had recognized his talents and would have felt himself a criminal to have not used them. It was then as he was deep in thought that the gang of toughs attacked him.

They had the triple advantages of surprise and numbers, and they were also completely familiar with their surroundings. As one pulled at Holmes's coat in an effort to pin his arms to his side, another punched him while the third tried to trip him. In a swift baritsu move he slipped from his overcoat and rushed to a wall. Then with his back safe from attack, he took up his classic boxer's stance.

'Oh, wot a toff. Who learnt yew 'ow to do that with yer mits?' guffawed one of his assailants spitting onto his hands before clenching his fists and advancing. He was by far the largest of the three and the obvious self-styled leader. Holmes knew what to do. A straight left removed his attacker's only good tooth and a rapier-fast right cross into the surprised face finished the encounter. The sidestreets consumed the others.

As he stepped out along Leather Lane nearing his rooms in Montague Street, Holmes heard the sound of a barrel organ playing a popular tune and a Cockney voice singing along to it. An Italian recently come from Naples was grinding the handle. He was gazing devotedly at the songstress. Beneath the caked make-up made more bizarre by the harsh limelighting of the organ lamps redolent of a painting yet to be brushed by a crippled aristocrat in Montmartre, Holmes recognized a zest for life that spoke of resilience and optimism. It was then that he felt it to be his vocation to protect that spirit no matter where it was harboured. Little did he know that one of his first cases would start exactly where he was standing, with me at his elbow.

Holmes was now resolved and it was that decisiveness that his brother recognized as he stepped back into their rooms. The undecided boy from East Anglia, late of Sussex, Montpellier and Oxford had become a man of resolu-'tion in London.

Holmes returned to Oxford and again tendered his resignation, which was again refused. There was no Gallic shrug this time, merely a steely determination to advance his plan. He had started at Oxford in October 1873 having spent his eighteenth year with his mother in Montpellier. Thus he was slightly older than most of the others in his year and that coupled with his seriousness gave an impression of greater age which made the others keep their distance. At least that was what Victor Trevor told me. I have often wondered whether Holmes did this on purpose as we both found him a most charming companion — as did my younger sister several years later.

Holmes would occasionally visit my family for dinner and he would usually end up the life and soul of the party. First my family would give him objects such as a hat, umbrella, dog-collar, or some such thing and ask him to explain to us what he could see in them of their history and their owners. Needless to say he quite dazzled everyone, including myself who was used to his ways by now. I wondered, briefly, if he was doing it to impress my sister, but he was not. Women just did not fit into his scheme of things. His mind had been made up on 23rd December 1874 as to the course in which his life was to run and he would no more be deflected by a well-turned ankle than by mortal danger to his person.

Once I persuaded him to play the violin at one of these

gatherings. It was a most moving piece that had us rapt in awe at its beauty and Holmes's virtuosity. He then played a jaunty air and we were restored to our high spirits, my father and I singing as my sister played the piano.

It was after dinner that evening that I prevailed upon Holmes to tell us the story of the *Gloria Scott*. During the story, which he recounted as factually as if he were reporting a scientific experiment, rather in contrast to Watson's telling of the tale, he mentioned that he had spent seven weeks of his first long vacation carrying out a few experiments in organic chemistry. I questioned him on this, asking him whether it was a hobby considering that it was not among his subjects at that time. He said that it could not really be described as a hobby, more as a complement to his theological studies. In answer to our obviously bemused looks he said that just as an apple is popularly believed to have led Newton to formulate the laws of gravity and as a consequence strengthen his faith in the existence of God, so Holmes had hoped to find God in the complex relationships of cells and their components. A universal law of organic chemistry would be proof indeed of the existence of God, he felt. It was typical of him to so off-handedly refer to these potentially earth-shattering studies as 'a few experiments.'

Holmes was certainly a seeker after truth in all his activities. I cannot help thinking of the Great Hiatus of 1891–94 which included a two-year visit to Tibet with a stay of some days with the Head Lama in Llasa for good measure. Some have felt that Holmes was not quite the same man after his return, although 1895 was a year which Watson felt to be one of Holmes's best.* (My personal choice as to Holmes's vintage year is 1889.) Thus some

Black Peter.

have concluded that while in Tibet Holmes had studied Buddhism and found its teachings influential on his subsequent behaviour. In support of this these commentators cite the sharp decrease in the mention of alcohol, tobacco, and in particular cocaine. As only one living creature was killed by Holmes after 1894 (*The Lion's Mane*), these critics regard their case as proved. I am afraid that I cannot agree with them. Whilst I agree that Holmes's best cases were before 1891 in the sense of originality and ingenuity of solution, there is a good reason for it. Moriarty was still abroad up to his tricks. As Holmes was to say later* the death of Moriarty had robbed crime, and the newspaper reports of it, of endless possibilities — 'with him in the field anything was possible.' Thus does it not follow that Holmes lost some of his enthusiasm for crime detection when his intellectual rival fell from the lists? With regard to Buddhism, Holmes had studied it at university as a comparative to Christianity. Such was his depth of knowledge of the subject that Watson was even to comment** that he spoke on a quick succession of subjects — including the Buddhism of Ceylon — 'as though he had made a special study of it.' With regard to Holmes's non-taking of life, have we forgotten his words in the *Three Garidebs*? When Watson was shot by 'Killer' Evans, Holmes assured Evans that 'If you had killed Watson, you would not have got out of this room alive.' Said in the heat of the moment? Perhaps; I keep my opinion to myself. Finally I would mention Holmes's addiction to cocaine. That he was addicted before the 1891–94 period is positively clear from the opening lines of *The Sign of Four*, and that there is no direct mention of cocaine in any of the cases after 1894 is equally

The Norwood Builder.
**The Sign of Four.*

true, but it does not follow that he was cured by a fresh study of Buddhism in Tibet during the Great Hiatus. Once again it is poor Watson not getting the credit he deserves in the partnership. It is clearly stated in the *Adventure of the Missing Three-Quarter* that Watson had gradually weaned Holmes from 'that drug mania which had threatened once to check his remarkable career.' Watson goes on to concede that Holmes now no longer 'craved this artificial stimulus under ordinary conditions' but, underratedly knowledgeable physician that he was, he knew that 'the fiend was not dead but sleeping.' How true that is of the addict! Obviously Holmes had to have the will to overcome his addiction but without Watson's guidance and assistance he would have found it a very uphill task indeed. As a conclusion to all this we must not forget the reference to 'occasional indiscretions of his own' which had contributed to his collapse in the *Adventure of the Devil's Foot.* Are we to infer the worst and believe that the fiend had fitfully woken?

However, I find myself digressing from my original thoughts on Holmes and the pursuit of truth. I do not know if his experiments led to enlightenment, to my knowledge he has never told anyone about his conclusions. Perhaps he is sharing them with his bees down in Sussex. What I do know is that his experiments gave him knowledge that was to prove very useful in his chosen career.

As I sit back and reflect on those events so long ago I have to smile. My sister had a typical schoolgirl 'crush' for Holmes which did not manifest itself in the usual way of dewy eyes and mooning looks but made her more adult as she tried to talk to Holmes as a 'grown-up'. Yet 'from the mouths of babes' etc. was certainly applicable in this case as my sister seemed to find out a great deal about Holmes's early life from their fireside chats. She concluded that Holmes's three greatest friends were Watson (obviously she must have spoken to me later about this as Holmes and Watson had not met then), Victor Trevor and myself. In all three it was a case of opposites attracting or at least complementing. In my case she said that Holmes had needed a friend when we had met in late 1878, not only to use as a sounding board for his theories after several years of intense research, but also because since Trevor's departure to the Terai he had become lonely — Holmes was only human after all. Possibly he had even doubted himself during those long years of few cases and little income. I was a catalyst if you like.

That's as maybe; woman's intuition, I suppose. I have my doubts, but as I say, my sister found out a great deal concerning Holmes's early life so I give her the benefit of the doubt. I shall now set out her information but in paraphrase as I could not possibly remember all her words — they were far more than Trevor's and spoken on several occasions many years apart. One other proviso must be that I do not know how accurate all this is. How much of it is impish humour by Holmes feeding a young female imagination and how much is 'woman's intuition' I do not know. Nonetheless here it is for you to judge.

Sherlock Holmes — The Early Years (by Miss Stamford)

The Holmes family seat was in East Anglia. It was to Holme Hope that grandfather Mycroft Holmes returned with his French bride. They made an unusual couple. He was powerful and every inch of his six feet six inches the traditional country squire with his dogs, shooting, fishing and healthy appetite. She was much smaller with a dark fine-boned beauty to his ruddy outdoor hue, a quickness in contrast to his deliberation, and a love of art in many of its forms creating a counterpoint to his rustic preoccupations. They were a marriage of opposites. (So that's where Holmes got his love of opposites I suppose, sister dear?) They had two children, both boys, Sherrinford and Sherlock. Sherrinford took after his father and was very much the country squire. Sherlock was more like the French mother. He married a local girl and they had two children, Mycroft and Sherlock. They all lived in the large house at Holme Hope.

The arrangement was not ideal. There can never be two mistresses in one home. On top of that it looked as if Sherlock's wife was more suited to Sherrinford, both of them being very much the country folk at heart. Sherlock senior on the other hand was very highly strung, not like a country squire at all. (In fact when Holmes talked about his family in *The Greek Interpreter*, he was careful to talk about his 'ancestors' being typical of their type, 'who appear' — is that significant? — 'to have led the same life as is natural to their class.' One does not usually refer to one's father as one's 'ancestor.' Neither was he actually the squire. Is he making a loophole for his father?) He loved music in particular and was very fond of cooking. Then of course there were the boys themselves. So different and yet so alike. Mycroft early retiring into his armchair with his mathematical problems, usually worked out in his head so that it looked as though he was doing nothing while he was engaging in strenuous mental activity. Sherlock the more active showing a keen interest in all around him but sharing also his mother's interest in the Bible and its lessons.

Unfortunately his precocity in that direction soon left his mother behind so that she was at once proud yet wary of her almost unnatural little boy.

Thus, taken from Holmes's mother's point of view, Holme Hope was a great disappointment, frustration and mystery.

There was the rivalry with the Grandmother Vernet — real or imaginary and the aloofness of old Holmes (who dies soon after anyway despite the family history of longevity). Then came the two brothers, Sherrinford and Sherlock. The one she should have married was like old Mycroft and tended to be distant from her, the other that she did marry was more like the French woman who was her rival. Did he give his loyalty to his mother in preference to his wife? Finally came her two children. Both were becoming strangers to her with their uncanny gifts and their own private games of numbers and guessing what people were. Although she was unsure about the word 'guessing' because they were so often right — at least Mycroft certainly was. In an earlier age they would have been burnt as warlocks — and old superstitions died hard in the heart of the countryside. Had the French woman brought something unnatural with her from 'over there'? Holmes's mother was a perplexed woman.

The last straw came when Sherlock, her baby, seemed to know more of the Bible than she who had solemnly studied it all her life with the slow tenacity of the country person, and seemed to leave her for his father to learn how to play the violin and prepare a dish that sounded as though it had rats in it — 'a rat or two', or some such name.

It was time to fight back. She now used feminine wiles such as preparing everyone's favourite food (when it had an English not French origin). When that failed to have the desired effect, she would change and become sharp and bitter, even to Sherrinford.

Eventually the house fragmented. Grandmother Vernet kept to herself and painted, or sang, or drew. Sometimes she would even go to visit her relatives in France. When she came back she would bring exotic presents for everyone which made Holmes's mother even more jealous of her.

(Mycroft would invariably tell her where these gifts had come from, whereas young Sherlock was liable to go into a reverie at the contemplation of such foreign gifts.) Sherrinford tended to spend most of his time shooting or fishing. He was out of the house more than he was in it. Was he trying to avoid his sister-in-law? Sherlock, senior, was drinking too much and becoming morose. He did not seem mindful of the bad example he was setting. The boys became withdrawn and seemed to be observing the panorama that was opening up before them. They tried to pacify their mother and indeed it often worked but sometimes she would become resentful of their attentions and say that it was a fine state of things when children treated their mother as though she were the child.

Then came the day when Mycroft left for university. He was being given advice from all sides as he boarded the train, but just as the train was leaving he looked out of the window and said to his parents: 'Before I go I have some advice for you both. Father, drink only to celebrate or to relieve insufferable tedium. Mother, travel — the broader the horizon the broader the mind. Both of you, visit France — and take Sherlock with you.' With that the train had pulled out before any reply could be made.

After much discussion it was agreed to visit the Vernets — without the grandmother.

Young Sherlock fell in love with France. Its sensations were so different and exhilarating for the Norfolk country boy. He felt stimulated by its very air. His favourite town was Montpellier but he resolved to visit all of France one day, particularly the warm south and south-west.

Sherlock's parents also felt something and fell in love but alas not with each other. The objects of their affections seemed quite perverse. The English mother fell in love with France and the half-French father fell in love with

Sussex as they travelled back from Portsmouth via Brighton. Both parents resolved to return to their new loves which resulted in the young Sherlock dividing his time between school in England (Winchester?) and holidays in France. He found this completely congenial to his tastes and made him a seasoned traveller, capable of packing a bag in five minutes, from an early age. Skills that were useful more than once later. His parents were now relatively happy. The father controlled his drinking and told his son about the many wines of France, in particular extolling the virtues of the great vintages of Bordeaux whose châteaux had been classified into groups of merit in 1855. Sherlock also learnt more of the violin and grew to love Sussex in preference to Holme Hope. Before long only Grandmother Vernet and Uncle Sherrinford were left there.

As to the mother she found the attentions of the French gallants much more to her liking after the tedium and tensions of Holm Hope. Sherlock merely shrugged his shoulders and observed that it was only natural for such a good-looking woman to have admirers. ('A sentiment expressed with regard to Miss Maud Bellamy in *The Lion's Mane*. Holmes obviously learnt young!' — Stamford.)

Many of Sherlock Holmes's later characteristics can be seen for the first time during this period. His love of the violin and knowledge of France are obvious. Mycroft's words of advice given from the receding window of his university-bound train also left a germ of an idea that bore later fruit. ('Surely he did not tell you about drugs, my dear little sister' — Stamford.) Also his attitude to emotional entanglements originate here. He had seen how an unhappy marriage could affect an artistic temperament and blunt, not hone, perceptions. His ascetic side had come out in his love of Bible study. Thus he could see emotional entanglements with the opposite sex could not be a help to his fulfilment. ('Do I hear a sigh?' — Stamford.) This does not mean that he became a woman-hater — he was quite aware of his father's failings and weakness of character which resolved Sherlock to be stronger himself. He was always chivalrous and courteous towards women, quite like a knight of old. It did not matter to him whether they were duchesses or destitutes, they were all damsels in distress to him. ('A rather romantic way of putting it perhaps, but then you would know more about that than I, sister dear' — Stamford.)

When he left school in July 1872, Holmes fulfilled the vow he had made to himself and travelled throughout France, particularly Bordeaux, Perpignon, Narbonne, Nîmes and Montpellier. In October 1873 he went up to Oxford.

From then until Christmas 1874 you know about, but what happened when Holmes returned to Oxford for the later term of 1875?

Once again his resignation was not accepted, and so he simply wrote to each of his tutors saying that he would be following a full course of study, but not with them. It was to be a syllabus of his own devising if they cared to peruse its parts — chemistry, anatomy, botany, geology, law, a little politics, and a new science which he called criminology. Again the whole gamut of academician twitches and tics became manifest, to no purpose. Holmes knew that non-attendance at lectures and tutorials was enough to earn him a dismissal so that the remaining two terms at Oxford had to be used to their fullest. Public lectures were attended, museums and collections visited, experiments undertaken, results collated.

One thing that he had learnt from his experiences on the night of December 23rd 1874 was the need for concealment, and what better concealment than that of disguise. He practised make-up, alteration in posture, mannerism, speech, demeanour. Sometimes he would follow an acquaintance through Oxford. One day he was spotted which angered him but helped to refine his technique. He was never caught out again. He perfected a way of having several disguises on his person so that he was able to change his persona as he went. Sterndale was to discover this in *The Devil's Foot*: Holmes — 'I followed you.' Sterndale — 'I saw no one.' Holmes — 'That is what you may expect to see when I follow you.'

When the time came to leave Oxford there was no animosity on either the side of the college or of Holmes. The college regretted losing such a capable student, Holmes regretted that Oxford could not accommodate him. However, bolstered by letters of recommendation from his tutors and the knowledge that Beethoven never got a degree from Oxford, Holmes returned to Mycroft and Montague Street to continue his studies at London University, then gaining a considerable reputation for work in the scientific fields. Add to that the museums, galleries and concert halls, as well as the many streets of London whose ways had to be learnt, and Holmes's choice of a second university becomes a formality.

Did Holmes ever visit the United States during these years? There are certainly indications in Watson's chronicles that he admired the United States and wished for a closer relationship between the USA and the UK. He speaks of the folly of a king and his minister which he hopes will not stop the quartering of the Stars and Stripes and the Union flag. Also in the story of *The Red Circle*, he appears to be fully *au fait* with American criminals and with the work of the Pinkerton Detective Agency so that he can quickly recognize the villain as big Gorgiano of the Red Circle and the Pinkerton detective (Mr Leverton) as the hero of the Long Island cave mystery. (I think that

Holmes was pulling someone's leg here — there are no caves on Long Island.) However, he never actually mentions a trip to the USA despite his many other journeys. As with so many things we need more data.

That he travelled between leaving Oxford in 1875 and meeting my brother in late 1878 there is no doubt, but it was mainly to France. Both his parents and his grandmother died during this period and the money raised by the sale of the Sussex cottage of his father and the possessions of his mother was enough to enable Holmes to continue his studies as an external student in London.

During this period he made many contacts with people throughout London and the mysteries that he solved he never called cases as such because they tended to be, in his words, 'run of the mill'. Not that he did not learn to respect such problems — often by their very featureless nature being quite difficult to solve satisfactorily. They were more in the line of apprentice pieces. The most important work that he was involved in was his studying of 'all those branches of science which might make me more efficient.'

He gave himself three years to become proficient in his chosen career — like taking a degree he said. He was aware of the importance of deadlines and how they should be kept. Thus his 'degree term' was complete in June 1878. If he were a doctor he would have put a brass plate by his door, but as he was the first consulting detective in the world he did not have a precedent to direct him — or restrict him. Instead he put discreet advertisements in the newspaper. He always said that the press could be very useful if used properly.

Perhaps the very strangeness of the new title put prospective clients off, but whatever the reason, his faith in his methods with regard to the efficiency of the press must have been sorely tried because the only replies he received were from private detectives wanting to know what he was up to. They were not particularly friendly and one could be forgiven for mistaking them for his quarry not his colleagues. This in turn made him realize that there was definitely a market for one of his discretion and skills, so although his advertisements had failed him, his youthful enthusiasm had not.

As he was so close to the British Museum he was able to use its peerless Reading Room for some very recherché study, which raised the eyebrows of some librarians and made those who sat next to him feel a little uneasy as to the nature of this solitary student in their midst. (I can imagine Holmes telling my sister this. He would sometimes indulge in diverting 'theatricals' to enliven his mind by playing small private jokes on other readers. If, for example, a clergyman was sitting next to him reading work on Christian morality, he would get a book out on Devil worship and place the title in a prominent position so that the unfortunate cleric could not fail to see it — and be discomforted. It was always the pompous who received this treatment, some of them either being or were to become rather prominent men.)

During this period of 'too abundant leisure time' certain cases did come Holmes's way 'principally through the introduction of old fellow students.' The third of these cases was the Musgrave Ritual, brought to him by his old friend Reginald Musgrave who had succeeded to the family inheritance at Hurlstone in Sussex two years before on the decease of his father. They had not met for four years and it was this case which brought Holmes the 'break', as Americans would say. The full details of the case are set out in Dr Watson's *The Memoirs of Sherlock Holmes*. As to the other two cases brought to Holmes's attention before this he would only give cryptic references.

Miss Stamford concludes: 'Sherlock Holmes drifted out of my life when my brother went on his travels and I stayed at home in Kent with my brewer parents. I had never forgotten him — one had only to read the newspapers to find evidence of his activities although I often felt that some of Scotland Yard's more spectacular successes seemed to owe more to him than was revealed in the newspapers. This does not mean that I doubted the abilities of the Scotland Yard detectives, but my own personal experience of his methods in finding my husband Neville St Clair for me in June 1889 proved to me that he is the greatest of detectives.'

Stamford Continues

So now you know the identity of my sister. It should also explain why he stayed with her in Lee, Kent, during the investigation of *The Man with the Twisted Lip*. It was out of friendship, not a romantic adventure. His words to Watson justify his presence there by saying that he had 'many inquiries which must be made out here' when in fact he had none, was another of his 'build-ups' to what he hoped would be a happy scene as surprising as it would be helpful to my sister and to Watson. He thought that as I had been Watson's dresser, that Watson would know my sister and be a friendly face among all the terrors of her predicament. That was why he wanted Watson to come along at such short notice, to help my sister as much as himself. It was typical of him to have set up the scene where the two old friends would meet. Unfortunately Watson did not know my sister as he had never met her. She had never been up to Bart's during Watson's time nor he back to Kent with me. As you know we were several years apart in age and not particular cronies then.

As to the other two cases that came along to Holmes's Montague Street premises, you may read them in the first volume of these papers.

We are now up to the latter months of 1879. The Musgrave case and particularly Musgrave's connection enabled more clients to find Holmes, and his time became increasingly busy. Several of his solutions to cases which had entirely fooled the regular force brought his exceptional talents to their collective attention and Inspector Lestrade was able to make use of his talents on many cases, particularly a very knotty one about a forger which Watson mentions in his *Study in Scarlet*.

Holmes's reputation was increasing and as it did he had to experiment even more as the cases he became involved in tended to be only the complex ones that appealed to his intellect.

It was in 1877–78 that I started at Bart's. In June 1878 John H. Watson became Dr John H. Watson and went to Netley to be trained as a surgeon for the Army. As I look back on it Holmes and Watson missed meeting by two days. Would history have been changed if they had met then and not in 1881? I am sure that they would have become great friends whenever they met, Watson was like that. From my point of view if Watson had not gone to Afghanistan and stopped a Jezail bullet I would not have become involved in this story in the way that I am, so I am glad that the meeting was postponed for three years.

The Attendant Three-Quarter

Those who take the date of the Battle of Maiwand, Tuesday, 27th July 1889, as the one fixed point in a changing age with regard to the life and career of John H. Watson MD, from which all else can be deduced are right to do so — up to a point. However, we must be mindful that the still waters of Dr Watson ran so deep that even Holmes admitted that he could not fathom his companion's depths. History is not simply the study of dates and chronology. Many an event would have passed unnoticed but for the remarkable qualities of the participants.

When I first met Watson he was a final-year student at Bart's before he became qualified in June 1878. He was a strongly-built man of middle stature, with a fledgling moustache, a square jaw and a thick neck. In other words he was perfectly proportioned to play rugby football.

Hospital rugby was well established by then. The first Hospital Cup had taken place in 1875 and had been won by the oldest club in the world, Guy's Hospital.

In the early seventies the teams had been twenty-a-side with thirteen in the pack of forwards, three half-backs immediately behind the pack, one three-quarter behind them, and three full backs making up the last line of defence. The forwards would push against each other in their attempts to win the ball. Sometimes these pushing matches would last several minutes at a time accompanied by shouts of 'Heave' from the crowds, and 'Push' from the packs, although the half-backs would bring a little more finesse to the proceedings with such remarks as 'Steady with it,' 'Not too fast,' and 'Keep it together.' It was not just the two packs who pushed together like this. On one celebrated occasion two individuals pushed each other in the 'in-goal' area behind the posts for several minutes much to the delight of spectators and team-mates alike. The idea was that the forwards would push through their opposite numbers and kick the ball on when they had broken through the opposition ranks. In the resulting follow through the attacking forwards (i.e. those going forward chasing the ball) hoped to gain ground, possession and points.

It was now that the backs came into play. The halves had to pick up or drop on the ball that had just been kicked through the scrum by their opponents. They had to be expert dodgers and runners. They played for themselves and tucked the ball under one arm so that they could hand-off the opposition with the other. Passing was frowned upon and looked on as 'funking'.

The single three-quarter was quite a star of the side having to cover the whole width of the field between the halves and the fulls. As he was the first real line of defence against the opposing halves he had to be fast and a fierce tackler. However, he was not expected to run with the ball but he did have to be an accurate kicker for touch and goal.

Finally, bringing up the rear were the full backs. They were there simply to defend and so they had to be expert tacklers, although in those days punting for touch was frowned on. It had to be drop-kicked which is more skilful.

During the seventies the game changed. The numbers on each side were reduced from twenty to fifteen, the first international with fifteen-a-side was England versus Ireland at the Oval on 5th February 1877. I was there and saw England prosper by two goals and a try to nil. There were now nine forwards and two of each of the backs — although the rules were not strict on that. The old, 'blind', shoving was replaced by the forwards trying to wheel the scrum, and then having got the ball at their feet and the opposition forwards on the wrong side they would charge downfield.

In 1878 the rules changed and a player now had to release the ball immediately he was held. As a consequence the best forwards were those who could include among their repertoire of accomplishments close dribbling, a fast follow-up in support, and quick accurate short passing. Above all they had to be fit.

The club that did the most to bring about this change in the London area was Watson's Blackheath. They even included two men in their 1878 pack who were there not because of their bulk or weight but because of their strength and speed off the mark away from the scrum either in pursuit of the ball or in support of the halves. These players tended to be of average height and thick-set. In other words, Watson to a tee. Big Bob Ferguson might have thrown Watson over the ropes and into the crowd at Old Deer Park when the former was three-quarter for Richmond, but it was Watson's style and team that was to carry all before them in the future. Ironically Blackheath's greatest season was when Watson was in Afghanistan, for in 1879–80 they had an unbeaten season in which they played sixteen, won fourteen and drew the other two.

When Watson returned from Afghanistan he said that his health was 'irretrievably ruined'. Some have taken this as simply the words of someone who was at a low ebb at the time but I think that there was more to it than that. Watson had been used to being very fit and active — you did not play for 'the club' in that golden era under Lennard Stokes without being a fine athlete. Now, as he returned from his army campaign, he was aware that his wounds would prevent him from playing top-class rugby again. It was Watson the athlete, not Watson the man who was looking on his health in such a poor light. A.E. Housman was to draw the distinction between athlete and non-athlete years later in his rather melancholy way when he spoke of the athlete knowing something of death before he actually died because he had already died a little when he had stopped playing his sport. Thus Watson was being factual, not dramatic.

John H. Watson was born in Northumberland but never really knew the place as his mother died shortly after his birth and his father took him and his brother south to stay with his sister and her husband. The stay there was only temporary as the three Watsons, father and sons, soon travelled to Australia in an effort to find fortune. Watson's father, Mr H. Watson, was a success in Ballarat* as a claims and land agent. This was a job which called for strength of character in the face of often armed adversity, but above all it called for honesty.

These qualities, as well as being prepared for action, were clearly passed to Watson 'minor'. However, the rough and tumble of frontier colonial life also passed on to John an appreciation of drink, women and gambling as well as the natural aptitudes for army life in the far-off stations of Empire.

So successful was Watson *père* that he was able to send his sons to school in England where John was to befriend

*In The Sign of Four Watson clearly recalls Ballarat from his youth.

Percy ('Tadpole') Phelps, 'a very brilliant boy' whose uncle was Lord Holdhurst, 'the great Conservative politician.'

The school was a natural one for a sporting youth — Rugby. Because Watson was two forms below Phelps it has been taken that Watson was rather a plodder. This is unfair. He had done remarkably well to overcome the deficiencies of a colonial educational background and earn a place at such an exalted school. Unfortunately from the academic point of view, Watson preferred sport to books and so tended to shine on the field, not in the classroom. Given what we know of Phelps from the 'Naval Treaty' he was a rather feeble and highly strung young man given to emotional outbursts of self-pity. I do not think Watson suffered by being two forms below 'Tadpole'.

It was during the holidays that Watson spent his time with his guardian, who was of course his aunt, in the south of England. Thus he fondly remembers the glades of the New Forest and the shingle of Southsea from his schooldays, a time of contrast to the impecunious spell he found himself in in later life which gave rise to his fond yearnings.

Watson's father died when he was still at school but there were sufficient funds to provide his brother with a legacy, including the £50 watch which Holmes was to use in his accurate deductions in the *Sign of Four* which offended Watson by their coldness (cf. Trevor at Oxford) and enough to defray the school fees for the remainder of Watson's education.

Watson's elder brother — also H. Watson — returned to Australia but was not the same success as his father. He lived in poverty apart from occasional periods of prosperity — these as a result of success in gambling on horses — at once a Watsonian and Australian failing. (I have known Australians bet on everything from the number of beans in a tin to the exact score in a Test Match innings.) He finally died of drink in Australia in 1885, the £50 watch passing to his younger brother as all that remained of his father and brother, the H. Watsons.

Watson clearly states at the beginning of *The Study in Scarlet* that he had 'neither kith nor kin *in England*' on his return from active service in Afghanistan. Thus we can assume that his aunt and her husband had both died and that his brother was back in Australia for the last years of his life.

What was Watson like as a student? He did not play rugby very often for the hospital — only in the Hospital Cup when needed. He was, as I have said, noted for his fairness and firmness by the dressers but we did not really mix with the finals boys. Not that that stopped us from playing tricks on them when using the cadavers. We would do such things as put mice into the abdominal cavity and wait for the reaction which was usually a case of the fainting finalist. Such tricks did not work with John H. Watson. He never fainted* — he had nerves of steel.

For his part he would tell us stories of life in Australia which would be a mixture of the picturesque and the bizarre. One occasion I particularly remember was when he told us about an Aboriginal ceremony called 'pointing the bone' in which the tribesman who had been found guilty of breaking their laws would be brought before the elders and a bone pointed at him with the result that he inexplicably died. It was a gloomy winter's afternoon and the gas lamps hissed a mournful wail and seemed not as bright as usual. His story soon had everyone in the dissecting room enthralled as he built up to the climax. He described the rituals and the staccato dances of the initiates as the condemned man

*Watson fainted only once in his life — *The Empty House*.

was brought before the elders and the final life-extinguishing bone pointing which left the victim writhing in agony before death took him. Just as he reached this point in his tale he pulled a fibula from the corpse on which he had been working and pointed it at one of the dressers who promptly fainted on the spot. After that we all thought him 'a good sport' and even more so when he treated us to a drink at the local public house — called 'The Butcher's Arms' of all names. For myself I was very impressed by his ability to tell a story and thought that he had a second career if doctoring failed to provide for him.

Despite these thoughts, Watson's choice of a career as an army surgeon seemed natural enough to one of his honest, healthy, patriotic instincts. (Colonial children were often more patriotic than the home-grown variety!) That his regiment was the Fifth Northumberland Fusiliers was a reflection of his birthplace which he would have had to have put down on his registration document at Netley. The army in those days felt that having 'home-town' members in a regiment improved morale. This was to reach its height in the First World War with the so-called 'pal' regiments which consisted of all the males of a certain location joining up together. On the credit side was the very high morale of these regiments, but that was more than outweighed by the terrible effects on local communities of the whole-scale slaughter of a complete generation of young men of one specific area. It was this which helped to give rise to the legend of the 'lost generation' of the First World War and the practice of recruiting 'pal' regiments was never resorted to again. Later Watson was to tell that it amused him being attached to the Fifth Northumberland Fusiliers as he had no recollection of that county — so much for military theories of regimental morale.

It was during these early army days that Watson got to

know Shoscombe and the horse-racing stables there, a knowledge that Holmes was to find very useful in later years so that he even called Watson his 'Handy Guide to the Turf.' On the debit side Watson's love of the Turf was to cost him half his wound pension.*

We now reach the Afghan campaign and the mystery of Watson's wound. Where exactly was he wounded? He clearly states in *The Study in Scarlet* that 'I was struck on the shoulder by a Jezail bullet, which shattered the bone and grazed the subclavian artery.' Yet he also wrote of a wounded leg in *The Sign of Four* — 'I had a Jezail bullet through it some time before, and, though it did not prevent me from walking, it ached wearily at every change of the weather.' Finally in *The Noble Bachelor* he writes of 'the Jezail bullet which I had brought back in one of my limbs as a relic of my Afghan campaign throbbed with dull persistence.' Holmes himself added a more precise location by talking of a 'damaged tendo Achillis' which all doctors and classics scholars will know is in the heel.

The answer to this conundrum is quite simple. During the withdrawal from Maiwand, Watson stopped to attend to a wounded soldier who had dislocated a shoulder by falling off his horse on the rocky outcrops of that area. In the dire circumstances Watson had to attend as best he could to his patient. Thus he laid him on his back and sat next to him bracing his feet against his comrade's body and pulling on his shoulder and arm with his hands, his attitude being similar to an oarsman in his boat. It was then that the murderous Ghazi fired from below the rocky outcrop. The bullet passed through the right leg injuring the Achilles tendon and then across his body before lodging in his left shoulder where it remained. To a rugby wing forward who

Shoscombe Old Place.

needs speed off the mark and the ability to push with the shoulder, the bullet could not have done more damage. His playing days were over and he knew it, hence his sentiments as to irretrievably broken health. By the time he had recovered from those injuries he would be too old to play to a high standard again. He had learnt something of death and, as a consequence, of life.

What light can I throw on Watson's famous *Knowledge of the Women of Three Continents*? It never ceases to amaze me how so many have got this all wrong. 'Knowledge' does not mean 'carnal' knowledge as so many imply. The simple observation of mannerisms of talk, dress and deportment all bring 'knowledge of women'; and as Watson had lived on three continents his observations came from the women of three continents. 'Making love' has come to mean something far more physical since Watson's time and so has the expression to have a 'knowledge of women'.

We must not forget that at all times Watson was chivalry itself to women, and his admiration of them is revealed by the number of times his writing is at its most descriptive when describing a woman. He was at first pleased and then aghast to hear of Holmes's/Escott's engagement to Milvertan's servant. He thought that she was being cruelly used. Even women who have little physical beauty still have nobility of bearing or some redeeming feature in Watson's eyes whether they are the mutilated Mrs Ronder or the at first unprepossessing Anne of the *Golden Pince-Nez*.

Watson was one of those characters who, like so many young men making their way in the world at that time, felt that they knew everything about women but blushed to the roots if one of them asked him to post a letter for her.

He also married only once, but more of that later.

Thus we are now back to early 1881 and the Criterion bar with Watson 'as thin as a lath and brown as a nut', wounded, without any friends, and with bleak prospects. I wrote earlier that I rendered Mr Sherlock Holmes a great service by introducing him to Watson and not vice versa. I sincerely meant it. Without Watson, Holmes would have become too cold and calculating. Watson was able to give him perspective. Holmes was even to agree with this by saying that he needed Watson so that he could use him as the whetstone for his mind by thinking aloud in his presence. He even went so far as to say that he was 'lost' without his Boswell.

The attraction of opposites, my sister would no doubt say. I suppose on the mental level that my sister would be right, but deep down they were similar in many ways. Both were chivalrous, honest, fair men who completely trusted each other — Watson because of his friend's great intellect, and Holmes because to him Watson was a symbol of all that was good and worthy of preservation and protection in a world where crime and injustice were without a true champion until the world's first consulting detective appeared on the scene.

The Dresser

Young Stamford I have been for so long that I shall remain thus and not enlighten anyone as to my proper forename. I rather like my eternal youth and as my forenames are rather prosaic it would add nothing for me to reveal them.

That I was Watson's dresser during his final year and the agent of the introduction of Holmes and Watson, you already knew.

That I came from Kent, the son of a local brewer, the brother of the wife of Neville St Clair (*The Man with the Twisted Lip*), you now know. There is much you still do not know and some of it I am loath to reveal, but as you will be reading this when I am dead there is no reason for me to hold back now.

Firstly, my appearance. As a young man I was rather shorter than Watson and also thicker-set. My face was round and ruddy and my hair was red with a curious lock of bright carrot hair at the front. Many people, particularly my barbers, recognized me for that one feature alone. I was rather heavy for my height so that I am quite pleased to be remembered as 'young Stamford'. To my contemporaries I was 'Stumpy', meaning short, or with the perversity of

English humour, 'Lofty'. One wag obviously well up on his history called me 'Harold's last victory' which was more difficult to unravel. I think 'Young' will do.

My next revelation is one that I make by way of a confession. I was Sherlock Holmes's source of cocaine. I had both the money and the access. Laudanum was still fairly freely available as a medicine on prescription and otherwise, but morphine and cocaine were decidedly more difficult. There were places — Jermyn Street was a regular place — but these sources were not really to be trusted. On the one hand it was not always of good quality (although Holmes was soon adept at refining it) and on the other, it left one open to blackmail. Cocaine was first brought to Europe in about 1750 but was not well known until its use in 1884 by the Viennese oculist Koller, and then only in medical circles. But by 1879 it was already well known to Sherlock Holmes. He had made a study of poisons as part of his self-imposed researches as early as 1876, and even Watson noted in early 1881 that Holmes was 'well up in belladonna, opium and poisons generally.' In fact it was one of the most well known features of him at Bart's. As Watson recorded me saying at the time, 'I could imagine his giving a friend a little pinch of the latest vegetable alkaloid, not out of malevolence, you understand, but simply out of a spirit of inquiry in order to have an accurate idea of the effects. To do him justice, I think that he would take it himself with the same readiness.' That was precisely what he had done, and as fortune would have it he took it at just the wrong moment. He had just completed a long series of experiments and researches but was still without a case. His mind needed something — alas it got cocaine.

There were no laws as such against cocaine and it is a great credit to Watson that he was so early aware of its dangers — another proof of Watson's abilities and learning.

However, what I was going to say was, as there were no laws against cocaine, why should the user be liable to blackmail? It is quite simple, the supplier of any addictive drug can have a strong hold over his client and his knowledge can be sold to others who might not be so sympathetic. It is a tightrope that all addicts tread at great risk.

It also makes a liar of the user. When Holmes and Watson swapped shortcomings as a preliminary to sharing lodgings, Holmes told Watson of his chemicals, experiments, violin playing, and getting in the dumps at times. Unless this last was a hint there is no mention of drug addiction. However, Watson was soon to notice that when Holmes lay idly on the sofa he had 'such a dreamy, vacant expression in his eyes, that I might have suspected him of being addicted to the use of some narcotic.' Watson the medic was spot on — Holmes had been addicted for two years that I know of. Yet Watson the chivalrous man steps in and concludes the above sentence by adding — 'had not the temperance and cleanliness of his whole life forbidden such a notion.'

It grieves me to use such words as 'liar' and 'addict' with reference to such a man as Holmes, but cocaine is as insidious and as deadly as any Moriarty and I must be blunt. As I look back through Watson's stories I see that Watson speaks of 'weaning him from his drug mania' but he was well aware that it could return, hence his blessing Cyril Overton's timely intervention by presenting him with the case of *The Missing Three-Quarter*. Watson all through shows himself as an enlightened practitioner way ahead of his time and as the loyalest of friends. I said that I had done Holmes a service by introducing him to Watson. It was the least I could do to atone for my other introduction. Perhaps I am too hard on myself. Such a resourceful man as Holmes would have found a source without me, but I still feel guilty.

I did not become addicted to its use — then. As a brewer's son I had another set of vices. Alcohol was my drug, as it was for many others. It was socially acceptable to be a member of a rugby team and drink to excess, particularly after a famous victory, than to be a Bohemian ascetic alone with a needle in a shuttered room. The one appears healthy indulging in 'harmless horseplay', the other somehow more sinister. It was my indulgence in 'harmless horseplay' that made me leave Bart's under a cloud and upset the lives of those I held most dear; whereas Holmes only ever hurt himself. They are both either guilty or innocent — there can be no compromise. Watson and his Beaune, Stamford and his ale are in the same dock as Holmes and his cocaine.

Talking of dock reminds me of what I should be talking about. I had had three years at Bart's and that was sufficient to be able to sign on a ship as a 'surgeon'. It was only a named appointment which involved a seaman's duties as the norm but a rapid transformation into a surgeon in time of crisis.

I had prepared myself for my voyage. My reefer jacket was thick and warm but I had a change of clothing for hotter climes. Pride of place in my sea chest went to my surgeon's bag with its highly polished instruments ready for action.

My plan was simple. I wished to sail around the world via Australia and I was sure that my skills would help me to achieve that end. If they failed I hoped that my Englishness would be able to fill the breach.

As a boy I had read stories of tea-clippers, the Horn, the Cape, becalmed, the Barbary Coast, Singapore, the South China Seas, whales and dolphins, giant squids, shipwrecks, junks, sampans, dhows, Magellan, Drake, Raleigh (my hero), and the Spanish Main. Would I meet a pirate? Would I make my fortune? What did the future hold in store for me? Holmes, Watson, family, everything was forgotten as I made my way to my ship. The morning was young and raw, flecks of snow spun helter skelter in the breeze, landing on my newly grown moustache. My nose was cold and as grey-blue as the Thames. The leather of my boots was hardened by the chill and they were like strangers to me. I held my ticket in my hand and searched along the quay for my ship. The *Stour* was nowhere to be seen. Rigging creaked, water plopped and sprayed, steam hissed but the *Stour* was invisible. At last I chanced upon a caricature. He was seated on an upturned shrimp basket, a dirty clay pipe between discoloured teeth. His white beard grey with grime, an eye patch giving him a piratical mein, his hooped black and white shirt, red necktie, white trousers (at least I presume that was the original colour), laceless boots, and heavy reefer a grandfather to my own, suggested a nautical calling. I asked him if he knew where the 'Stour' was anchored. First he asked if I was a bat. Next he chuckled and spat a large residue of chewing tobacco at a cockling gull near his foot. Finally he pointed. I looked over my shoulder and my heart sank. Between two fire vessels bound for Bombay was a dirty single-stack barge — the *Stour*. This was my first 'ship'.

I could not believe my eyes. As I stood agog, a foreign timbered voice cried up to me, 'Mr Stamford?' I nodded my response. 'First stop Amsterdam.'

I will never forget that voyage. All that I had learnt of anatomy went overboard — in more ways than one. My heart was in my boots, my stomach was in my throat, my head between my knees, and my sea legs were still to be fashioned.

After a day of pitching and tossing, rolling and yawing my spirit had all but left me. My breakfast had long gone.

The cook, an apparition of oil, jocularity and individual aroma, prepared one of his 'specials' for me. Bacon has never been my favourite meat, and streaky back my least favourite cut. The medicine did not work. After several hours I managed to get a grip on myself and make the first steps in time with the movement of the ship. This gave me confidence to go on deck.

I staggered to the rail and looked over the side. Breathing deeply I felt my strength returning. A seagull flew inches from my ear and I looked up. Momentarily I took my hands from the rail and paid no attention to the rhythm of the ship. The horny hand of a Dutch sailor held on to my collar. 'No yet, Surgeon. Ve may haf need of you, ja.' He smiled at me and was gone about his business. A near miss, I thought.

I tried to take my bearings. So this was the North Sea. It was green and grey, stippled with dirty spray. Its salt was on my lips and in my eyes. Surely I had not wept. Octavian at Actium and Nelson just about everywhere had been seasick. The company might be impeccable but the nausea was still the same. I concentrated on the sea. It made me worse. The depths were solid grey moving in one direction, the surface was lifeless green moving in a counter direction. The foam flicked and sprayed at all angles. The movements of the grey and green had a rhythm all their own, sometimes largo, sometimes staccato, but whether slow or fast it was impossible to follow them. My head throbbed with the efforts; my eyes felt as though they had crossed and recrossed. I closed my eyes to escape this torture — yet still my mind's eye grappled with the problem of the conflicting rhythms. The tighter I screwed my eyes, the more my head pounded. My legs were no longer my own. The wind chilled me. The sea beckoned me, a cruel siren already acclaiming her victory. My feet slipped beneath me, but my hands gripped the rails. I tried to breath with regularity. I felt as though a forty-man scrum was on my chest. My head started to nod in the first stages of lost consciousness. The netting held me on deck, but for how long? The pulsing rhythm of the grey-green was calling me down.

'That was a bad moment, Mr Stamford,' said a solemn voice. Solemn out of striving to make itself understood in a language not its own — its natural note seemed cheerful.

I looked around me. 'Where am I? What happened?' my voice feebly inquired; my throat parched and sore with its savage usage.

'The crew's quarters. It is eight of your clock, in the evening,' replied the voice.

My head could not limp a reply. I felt a strong hand on my shoulder. 'Not to worry. Even Octavian at Actium had his Agrippa, and your Nelson had his Hardy.'

I tried a witty response. It came out, 'Grr-ar-gh-grr.'

'You must have missed the company's wire. We were scheduled to go up the coast to Newcastle and you would meet a boat for Hamburg. As it is we go instead via Amsterdam. The North Sea is the worst part. The Baltic is not so bad — usually.'

So that was my first day at sea. It was an experience that I have never forgotten, and was never allowed to forget in future whenever I met Hans Rugler and his brother, Carel.

There is much to tell but little that is of any real consequence from the point of view of Holmes and Watson. I will therefore only sketch my travels but bring into sharper relief those incidents which will create some thread of continuity for my dealings with Holmes.

You don't need me to tell you about Rembrandt's town on the Amstel with its canals, barges, gables and raffish life mixed with stolid respectability. Suffice to say that I was charmed by it immediately. The Rugler brothers took me to various places that only sailors go and I learnt about the Far East and met Malays, Indonesians and natives of lands that I had never even heard of. What impressed me most was how the natives seemed to mix. The rather heavy, ruddy Dutch and the dark, finely boned Asiatics made beautiful half-breeds — a term which none resented. I started to learn the patois of the sea although it never became second nature to me.

After several days we set off for Hamburg and another set of experiences all of which were dwarfed by the enormity of my ship, the *Pompadour*. It had four masts and enough sail to cover half a dozen rugger pitches. The final provisioning and setting in of cargo had been finished that morning and we left on the next tide.

The captain was a German, Dieter Netzer. He was a wonderful man. A giant but truly gentle. He could do anything from haircuts to surgery, from fiddle playing to being judge and jury. He was that rare creature — a master of all trades. I asked him why they needed a surgeon as he seemed more than capable from what others had told me. He shrugged his massive shoulders (I would have to teach him rugby, I thought) and said that it was part of his company's regulations to have a proper surgeon so a proper surgeon they must have. Like so many of his race he stuck by the rule book most methodically. The new apprentice sailors would be grateful for this for he was a very thorough teacher and none dared cross such a strong man. Within a week, sailors from a dozen races, including myself, had learnt all the different names of the ropes, rigging and tackle in German and English.

Captain Netzer seemed to take a shine to me when I climbed up some rigging to bring a boy down after he had got caught up in some ropes and broken his ankle. That evening we chatted over a pipe and he gave me some of his mixture which soon had me coughing, much to his delight. 'That will put hairs on your chest, yah,' he chatted good humouredly. By the time we reached Valpariso we were firm friends.

Our journey round the Horn was not as fearsome as that first day in the North Sea, and the Pacific lived up to the name that Magellen had given it until we reached the mouth of the harbour when a real gale blew up. It was here that the captain showed his skill at the helm and brought us safely in without any assistance from the small lead 'tug' boats. Quite an achievement, I can tell you.

My original plan was to sail from Valpariso to Melbourne but I fell in with some Americans and decided to try my luck with them, which resulted in my going to San Francisco and Drake's Bay. The plaque was still in place then, I think it's lost now. Fisherman's Wharf and the Barbary Coast were pretty wild places where you could find yourself crimped and on your way to some unknown destination as a deckhand if you did not keep your wits about you. Fortunately the old shellbacks I knew had a ship already lined up for Yokohama.

Crossing the Pacific was not without event and landfalls were very welcome. Yokohama was even more welcome. I would often watch the fishermen in the harbour with their trained cormorants diving for a catch. What beautiful birds they were. At Yokohama I met up with my next English ship, an English mail boat which travelled the seas like a small 'Flying Dutchman' never stopping anywhere for long. Hong Kong and Singapore were my next ports of call, and in the latter I enjoyed great hospitality because my name tended to be confused with that of Sir Stamford Raffles and I was presumed a relative despite my not too great denials. Next came Rangoon, Bangkok and Calcutta.

It was during this voyage that I had some trouble and

was obliged to change my name and dye my hair in order to escape. It was a private operation for a rich Chinese. It failed and he wanted my head in compensation. Not a pleasant experience.

I was still unnerved as I reached Calcutta and so decided to keep to my new name of Surgeon Stewart.

It was here that I decided to look up one of Holmes's few old friends and so I took a small steamer up the Ganges to the Terai.

The Terai is a fairly flat land between the Ganges and the Himalayan foothills. It used to be rather marshy, over-grown with long coarse grass and infested with malaria. It was very much a frontier area then, not much populated or properly cultivated, but every so often one would come across some beautifully terraced areas that some enterprising planter had cut out in order to grow tea.

At the club in Pilibit after having been going up river for some two weeks I came across a large figure who looked sombre as he read a newspaper a year out of date. He had lost much of his hair and seemed prey to depression despite his full red cheeks.

'New member?' he asked cordially, if stiffly.

'No, but I have some more recent newspapers than the one you have been reading.' Among Englishmen in the tropics newspapers were often more precious than gold. He smiled and held out his hand.

'Trevor's the name. Got a plantation a few days away.'

I could not believe my luck. It had been so easy as though we had been infallibly drawn together. I introduced myself and before long the name of Sherlock Holmes came up in conversation. The name was like a magic formula, and in minutes we were chatting as though we had known each other for years. Later he took me to his plantation, the most isolated of them all actually, part of the Himalayan foothills themselves. It was then that he told me the story of the *Matilda Briggs*. Even thousands of miles away from Baker Street in a land trodden only by a handful of Englishmen, Sherlock Holmes was a profound presence.

When Trevor's tea had been loaded I took the steamer back to the delta where I boarded — the *Matilda Briggs*. It was with a certain amount of trepidation that I did so and I kept an eagle eye out for rats. My plan was to go to Bombay and pick up a clipper, and thus return to England via the Cape. However, before I had reached that great city I had fallen in love and jumped ship. Her name was Kerala, the nearest place on Earth to the Garden of Eden or Paradise. Lush palms undulated next to perfect blue seas. All the trees were laden with the riches of succulent fruit. The winds from the sea wafted ashore and the rains kept everything fresh. Trade in spices was a source of great wealth particularly at the British-administered Tellicherry. My skills as a surgeon were called on by the many races and religions who lived together in complete harmony. Before twelve months were over I was on my way to becoming a wealthy man. I made some investments and they prospered, but my main source of income was with my surgeon's knife. I still called myself Stewart just in case my Chinese enemy should hear of me again and come after me. Unfortunately for me he did and I had to make my escape in the dead of night with very few possessions in my haste. I then went to Bombay. I took the mail steamer back to England again, working my way as a ship's surgeon.

It was on this trip that I met a nurse named Carolyn Foggarty. Apparently she had come over with a large group of unattached eligible young ladies in the autumn, whose prime concern was to find a husband in the British community — military or civilian — in India. This was called by the military in particular the 'Fishing Fleet'. Those who were not able to find suitable matches returned to England in the spring and were cruelly labelled the 'Returned Empties'. Carolyn told me that several, including herself, had made the trip more than once and tended to be bitter at the many whispered barbs of humour. She had been sent by her father who was a mill owner in Lancashire. He wanted her to find a suitable husband which meant to him one who had good business connections on the sub-continent so that he could expand his operations there. There was talk of some brothers on Trincamalee, but that's another story. As she was a rather spirited girl she did not take kindly to her father's manipulations of her future happiness and so tended to resist her suitors. This resistance included flattening her vowels, dropping her aitches and emphazising her above-average height.

Carolyn told me of her desire to nurse and of her work at the hospital for the poor in Bombay. She so wanted to do something useful with her life. Her father would have said that that meant being a dutiful daughter and doing as she was told so that he could become a millionaire and in time a peer of the realm. Her interpretation begged to differ.

Despite the disparity of our appearances, she tall and thin, myself short and stocky, we felt relaxed in each other's company. Before long we sought each other out. By the time we reached the Canal we had become inseparable. At Port Said as the topees were ritually thrown overboard by those who were returning to England for the last time, we became engaged and at the other end of the Mediterranean our engagement ended as the captain married us in the shadow of the Rock.

By the time we eventually arrived in Liverpool word had reached Carolyn's father. To say that he was displeased that his designs had been thwarted and his daughter married to a penniless, unqualified ship's surgeon would be to misunderstand the temper of a Lancashire entrepreneur of the late nineteenth century. After some harsh words in which my newly acquired nautical vocabulary enabled me to trade as good as I received from my industrial critic, Mr Foggarty came grudgingly to admit the legality of our union.

He even attempted to draw me into his employ as I was a 'man of the world' in his eyes. Unfortunately for him my eyes were on Liverpool's university which as a part of the centre of trade for West Africa as well as the many parts of the British Empire had interested itself in the problems of that area. West Africa was indeed the White Man's Grave. It took a higher toll of British life than even the unhygienic slums of the great metropolitan centres of the Motherland. Thus my wife and I studied there until we became qualified and began our work to find a cure for the ills of that part of the Empire.

We lived in West Africa for eight years and had three children of our own, but countless adopted darker-skinned children thronged to our makeshift surgery and the care of my wife in particular. The Negro must be the most ingenuous, spontaneously warm person in the world. In England Carolyn and I were the 'Magnets', i.e. the opposites that had attracted. In Africa our attraction was somehow more heartfelt although my wife's rather awkward inelegance made us all laugh at times. This she took with such good grace that all loved her even more. It was as though she were trapped in a body which so inadequately expressed her inner beauty. She would sometimes see herself as a woman of mystery and intrigue with assignations awaiting her on the Orient Express, or as a Bohemian artist in Montmartre, or as an intrepid explorer — the first woman to enter Mecca or sail around the world single-handed. All who met her grew to love her. Her singing around the campfire was more enthusiastic than polished but everyone's face shone with delight nonetheless.

But I lose myself. I am writing of Holmes, Watson and that spear carrier Stamford. Carolyn was last to see me when she returned to Liverpool one winter (1890 to be precise, as though precision matters with such a timeless thing as this) to visit her father who was ill. I remained to look after our work in Africa. The father recovered, but Carolyn, now unused to English winters, contracted pneumonia and lies forever in a quiet English field that is now designated as part of the 'green belt'. I believe that there are plans to build what is called an 'A' road through that 'green belt' now. So much for designations.

I intended to return home, but travel then took so long that it was pointless. I comforted myself with grog and work, the latter proved a greater antidote to sorrow than the former until I realized that I would never find a cure for the diseases that I wished to conquer with my primitive equipment. Grog then became my solace and my torture.

M'twali, a man of great dignity and wisdom, told me to leave Africa because I was destroying not only myself but my wife's work as well. 'Go to that Paradise of which you speak when you have had your many drinks,' he advised.

Several months later I was kissing the sands of Kerula as my three children looked on in embarrassment. Yet 'In Arcadia, ego' proved to be the story of my earthly Paradise as my three children — James, Andrew and Felicity Carolyn — succumbed to the climate (how ironic!) and lack of a mother's love. That must appear fanciful now, with Fleming's penicillin as the cure-all, but then we knew little more than the local witch doctors. The only difference was that we wore white coats and washed our hands before as well as after an operation.

No challenge was too great for me now. I sought out Kuru in Guinea and like the three topers in Chaucer's *Pardoner's Tale*, I found him under a tree with his friend

Death. Perhaps my year in the tropics saved me, or possibly I was too pickled in Naval preservative to be fully affected, but that dreadful disease of the nerves killed all around me but left me to my life sentence.

Despite my wild behaviour and unkempt look, for some reason I remained popular with hard-drinking planters and eccentric missionaries. A Liverpool accent might have a very bad effect on my humour when I was in my cups but my surgeon's hand remained as steady as ever. However, I was game for anything and eventually got shipwrecked and washed ashore in China.

All that visibly remained of my past life was my reefer jacket that I had first worn so proudly as I had stepped upon the *Stour* that day in 1881. It was then that I started thinking of Holmes, dead in the Reichenbach Falls perhaps, but not forgotten. I took to opium, cocaine when available. For Holmes the latter had eased his boredom, for me it blotted out my memories. I was addicted. I will leave my other tales . . .

Several years later one of those double-edged things came to pass. It was 1897, Queen Victoria's Jubilee. I had a hankering to see London again, but no means of achieving my goal. Sign on as a ship's surgeon perhaps, but I had lost confidence in my ability with the knife in my addiction. Fate was to hold my hand. I went to an American Club in Shanghai (I was banned from the English ones) and read the newspapers. For some reason a copy of the *Manchester Guardian* was there. Naturally I chose to read that in preference to the *San Diego Charger* or the *Seattle Sounder*. In the personal columns was an advertisement asking for the whereabouts of a 'Surgeon Stamford' late of 'Keralu'. The name given was Mrs Eileen Foggarty — my wife's mother.

A month later I was at the club again with a ticket to England in my pocket. Old Foggarty had died and his wife had wished to trace me with a view to bringing what remained of the family together again.

1897 was a great year for me. I saw the Jubilee, was reunited with my family both of blood and in-law, and felt that a new start beckoned. I had not reckoned with my addiction. No matter what I tried it still haunted me. I thought of seeing Holmes or Watson again but somehow felt out of place. I returned to Liverpool to continue my studies of tropical diseases and help to look after the cotton mill of my in-laws.

I tried to become a respectable man of local affairs but always I felt that I would betray myself by an involuntary gesture or flush or stutter of speech or any one of a thousand ways in which the drug addict reveals himself. Slowly I weaned myself from the most serious addiction — mainly through reading Watson's accounts of Holmes's adventures and his recovery from his dependence. Often I too wished for a Cyril Overton to appear to dash temptation from me when the mood was on me. I was not always so lucky!

When the Great War started in 1914 I felt that my last chance had come to make amends for my indiscretions. To be exiled to the freezing North Atlantic was what I needed. I lied about my age — not that I really needed to — and was taken on.

As the war entered its final phase I was tired of being shot at by U-boats, I wanted to fight back. I was really too old for the Senior Service as such so I joined the Q-ships. I joined up with the *Ready*, a brigantine square rigger in the North Sea, and met someone I had first come across many years before in Singapore. He was a Pole by birth but was now called Conrad. We had to laugh — he was far older than I was and had been ashore for longer than I had. He saw no action on his tour. He had not changed much I thought as I saw his back receding down the gangplank for the last time — as taciturn as ever. Perhaps all great thinkers have to be like that, and it was not long before Holmes was on my mind again.

My last tour saw action. Our decoy tactics worked and we enticed not one but two U-boats to the surface expecting easy pickings. We threw off our disguise and sank one of them. That was my swansong at sea as it were.

The bar of the Criterion was a welcome and safe harbour.